# Trust on the Precipice

By

## Ronna M. Bacon

Verses

Ps 18:2

The LORD is my rock, and my fortress, and my deliverer; my God, my strength, in whom I will trust; my shield, and the horn of my salvation, and my high tower.

Joshua 1:9 Have I not commanded you? Be strong and of good courage; do not be afraid, nor be dismayed, for the Lord your God is with you wherever you go."

New King James Version

Dedication

To my Dad, who believed in me and showed the quiet confidence and strength needed for a daily walk with God.  Luv you, Dad.  Miss you.

Table of Contents

# Prologue

The men watched the couple and their children move around their campsite, wanting them to leave but not knowing how to make them move. It wasn't an illegal campsite, but it was on private property, property the men had no right be on. They conversed quietly, anger colouring their words. They had a delivery to make tonight, and this family was in their way.

The father moved towards them, not seeing them. He gave a quick cry as he saw them and turned to run, not getting far before he was on the ground, his arms bound. The men moved towards the family, quickly taking control of the two children and forcing the woman to come with them, threats to her children driving her.

They forced them into a vehicle and then drove them from the site, arguing in low voices what to do with them. The younger man didn't want to kill them, he said. That wasn't right, not a family. The older man, hardened from a life of crime, had killed before. Lives didn't matter to him. What mattered with his money. He had to make that delivery tonight.  A sudden movement by the man behind him sent the vehicle swerving across the road and into a ravine.  The vehicle spun, the backend hitting the rock wall, crushing it and sending the two men in the front seat through the windshield to the ground.  They lay for how long before they picked themselves up, broken bones, cuts and scrapes.

They stared at the vehicle, then one another.  This was not how it was to end.  How did they explain what had happened?  The younger man, hurt less than his cohort, reached into the vehicle, shaking his head at the older man, who cursed, his broken arm tucked into his shirt.  Now what, he thought?  How did they get right of the bodies?

Arguments broke out before they finally agreed on a plan.  The bodies were moved, the vehicle torched and they left.  Where they had placed the bodies, no one would find, they were sure.  They were from outside the area, no one likely knew exactly where they were.  They headed back to the campsite, gathering up everything and tucking it away in the family car before leaving in it.  They would get rid of all the evidence where it wouldn't be found.  Then they would return to make their delivery.  The van had been left on a little used road while they had scouted out the area.

Their plan seemed fool proof but was it?  That would be a question only time could answer.

# Chapter 1

Hand on her head, Caralee Lawson stared around her family-owned and run camp, Haven Camps, and felt a chill running through her body. Why, she had no idea. She just knew they had a lot of work to do to get the camp back up and running and with only two months to go, she wasn't even sure it was possible. The tornado that had ripped through the camp three days ago had destroyed a number of buildings and levelled many trees.

She turned as she heard steps crunching up beside and her brother stood there, his arm coming out to hug her. They were close, these two, only eighteen months apart in age. Nigel looked after his sister, sometimes to her dismay. He looked around before he spoke.

"There's a lot of work to do, Cara. Dad has spoken to the board and they're going to set up a work bee for this weekend to see how much debris we can get rid of." He sighed. "It's the cabins. Corin has taken a look at them. We have two totally demolished or gone. Three are heavily damaged and will need to be rebuilt. That leaves five with some damage and two that escaped any damage at all."

She sighed. "That's what I thought, Nigel. How do we ever open up again in time?"

"God provides us a way. You know that. We'll get there. Dad says he's planning a staff meeting for later today." He turned as his friend, Corin O'Rourke, approached.

Corin hesitated before he finally approached the siblings. He felt the animosity that sometimes came from Caralee and he wasn't quite sure why. He had met her over the years, been a guest in their home, but still there was just something that he couldn't put his finger on, some hesitation towards him. Lord, I have to work with this family and we can't if this continues. You'll have to work it out, that for sure.

"Nigel, do you have some time to go over the cabins? We should. That way I can do up an estimate for the board and have it ready."

Nigel nodded, swinging Caralee around to face the cabins. "Come on, sis. You've been wanting to make some changes. Now's the time to do so. With the cabins we need to rebuild and repair, you can let Corin know what you want to do. I know you've been planning on this at some point."

Cara sighed to herself. Of course, she wanted to do just that but to work with Corin? That she wasn't quite sure about, but maybe if she got to know him better, it would help. *Lord, You've allowed this. We need to trust You in this, because I sure don't know what Your plans are. I feel like I'm perched on a high cliff and ready to fall, without a parachute or bungee cord to stop me.* She peeked around Nigel and spotted Corin watching her, a half-smile on his face. She nodded.

"Okay, Nigel. Which one do we start with?" Corin spoke as he shifted his gaze towards the cabins.

"Which one, Corin? You've assessed them all. Which would you suggest?"

"What names did you have for them again?"

"We didn't really. Just numbers. Why?" Nigel walked around fallen branches to reach the first demolished cabin, his brow furrowed as he puzzled through what Corin had asked.

"I think naming them would be good. Cara, did you come up with names for them?"

She nodded, her eyes distant as she looked around. "I did. I have the names written down in my notes back at the house. I can get them to you later. This one, this was my favourite. I wanted to name it The Lookout. It stands alone, and you can see so far around it."

"I like that." Corin paused beside what remained of the cabin, which wasn't much. "Don't step in here, Cara. I'm not sure what is in this debris." He stared at the centre of the cabin area, now down to the dirt. "Nigel, do you have a shovel?"

"Why?" Nigel brought his attention back to Corin and stepped closer. "What's there?"

"I'm not sure." He turned to see where Cara was, his voice dropping as he spoke more quietly to Nigel. "It looks as if at some point someone has dug up this area. It's strange that it's underneath a cabin. How long have the cabins been here?"

"I'm not sure. Years at least. I know Dad did repair work on the floor of this one and the one next to it about fifteen years ago. I'll be right back."

Cara watched her brother walk away and then turned to Corin. "What are you thinking is down there?"

"I'm not sure, Cara. Nothing, I hope." He paused for a moment, his eyes catching sight of something white and his heart sank. "Cara, we need to move away from here." He moved towards her, his hand reaching for her arm.

She stared at him for a moment. "But why? Aren't you going to dig up the area?" She frowned as he shook his head and moved her further away from the cabin, back towards the tree line.

"No, I'm not. When Nigel comes back, I'm sending him for the police chief."

"Corin, you're scaring me. What did you see?" She twisted away from his grasp and ran back towards the area, Corin on her heels.

"Cara! No! Don't go in there!" He caught up to her, wrapping his arms around her waist and turning her away from the area, even as she struggled to get away.

"Corin? What are you doing?" Nigel slid to a halt, his eyes on his friend and his sister.

"Nigel, you'll need to bring in the police. We wouldn't be working this area for a while."

"And why not?" Nigel stabbed the shovel into the ground and approached them. "What did you find?"

"A bone. Nigel, I think there's a body buried under there." Corin felt Cara sag in his arms and he held her tighter.

"A body?" Nigel's voice rose to a squeak in his shock. "You're sure? Of course you are. You won't make that up." He turned. "I'll go find Dad and send him this way. Then I'll have to head for town if we still don't have phone service." He sighed. "Make yourselves comfortable. It's going to be a long day."

They watched as Nigel stalked away, hands waving in the air as he talked to himself. Cara wrapped her arms around herself and moved away from Corin.

"Cara?"

She turned to find Corin beside her, handing her his jacket. She shook her head, but he still wrapped her in it, feeling the softness of her dark brown hair as it brushed again his fingers, watching her amber eyes as they became shadowed at what the discovery would mean.

Cara looked up in the slate gray eyes of Corin, noting the dark shadow already on his cheeks, and the black curls he kept close cropped. "Corin, did you really find a bone?"

He nodded. "I pretty sure I did. They'll call in a medical examiner to make sure. But we won't be working around here for a few days." He heard her soft sigh. "It's okay. That will give us time to look at your plans and make some decision as to what you folks want."

She nodded, then turned with a frown as she heard the pulsating motor of a bike. "Who's out here? This is private property and we don't have any bikes out this way."

The sound grew louder and then stopped for a minute. Corin spun in a circle, trying to determine just where the bikes were. There was more than one, he thought. Then he caught the glint of sunlight on metal and grabbed at Cara's hand, his grip tightening on hers as she pulled and struggled to get free, his jacket dropping from her shoulders.

"Cara. Come on. We need to get out of here. Don't struggle, please. Hold on to me." He pulled her into a run, hearing the sound of the bikes starting up and growing louder. "Where can we go?" He shot a quick look behind him, then at her.

"Ahead and then to the left. We can get on a path there that will lead us into the forest.

It's overgrown, so I don't think they can get through." Her breath came in gasps as she struggled to keep up with Corin.

"No!" She looked ahead as Corin let out a yell. They had been cut off on the left and the only way to go was to the right.

"Not that way, Corin! No! Not that way!" Cara tried to pull him back with her, but heard the whine of the motor close behind them. "No! Dear Lord! Don't let us fall, Lord! Please!"

Corin heard her frantic pleas and not knowing the area, didn't realize the danger they were being chased into. He felt the ground begin to give under his feet and he tried to throw them backwards but the bikes were too close behind them. He did the only thing he could at that point. He reached and wrapped Cara in his arms, and threw himself sideways, not knowing what he was falling into but determined to protect her from as much hurt as possible. He felt his body hit the sharp rocks and brush. Then his head bounced off a rock and his vision darkened. Lord, please let me hold onto Cara. Help me to protect her. Their bodies rolled a few times until Corin landed on his back and then slid down the hill, rocks and debris following. A few stones peppered them as they came to a rest near a creek.

Dust settled on the ridge as the two bikes stopped, the men clad in black with full face helmets. A few words and gestures and they were on the way, confident they had solved their problem. They didn't see or hear the ATVs bringing Nigel and his father back to the area.

Nigel stared after the bikes, before looking around. "Dad, where are Corin and Cara? I left them right here."

His father, Bruce, looked around, spotting the footprints of the two overlaid with the bike treads, and then Corin's jacket, tread marks running across it. "There. They were chased." His eyes raised and his face paled. "Nigel! The cliff. Don't tell me. Please not that!"

They jumped from their ATVs, leaving them back far enough from the edge that they wouldn't send anything more over. Bruce grasped Nigel's hand and leaned over, his heart in his mouth as he saw the two bodies, Cara still wrapped tight in Corin's grasp.

"They're down there, Nigel. We need to get to them, but we need help."

"You go down by the old path, Dad. I'll go call for help." He paused, his face white, his eyes pleading with his father. "Are they moving?"

"I can't see that well. Go, Nigel. Bring the radios when you come back and the emergency supplies that we'll need." He looked up at the sky. "It's getting colder and those clouds look like rain. We'll need to keep them warm and dry. Go, son, now."

Bruce watched as Nigel ran for the machine and then headed off at a reckless speed before he headed along the brink of the cliff to an old path and down it, reaching the two in short order. His hands on them, he paused for a moment to pray, then feeling for breath sounds and heartbeats. His head dropped in relief. They were alive but how badly injured, he had no idea.

# *Chapter 2*

$\mathcal{N}$igel stood at the brink of the cliff, watching as the emergency personnel hurried towards his father. He prayed as he had never prayed before. He couldn't lose his sister. Nor his best friend. Lord, please. Help me to trust You in this. He had been down to his father when he returned and been sent back up to watch for the men and women who responded. He could hear his father's quiet conversation with them, but couldn't catch the words.

Soon enough, the first stretcher, the one with his sister, was carried up and over to the waiting ambulance, Nigel following closely. He watched as her eyes flickered and pain traced across her face.

"Nigel?"

He crowded close, ignoring the looks he was given by his friends working that day. "Cara?"

"We were chased, Nigel. Two men on dirt bikes." Her voice was low and pain filled even as she faded away again.

Nigel felt the hand on his arm as the police chief, John Gregory, pulled him aside. "Let them work, Nigel and then get her to the hospital.  What has she said?"

Nigel stood in a way he could watch his sister and watch the cliff, anxious for news on his friend. He spoke to the tall gray haired chief, a cousin of his father's.

"Just that they were chased.  That's what we thought when we saw the tracks. Two men, she said, on dirt bikes.  Whoever it was had to have known the area, to chase them that way." Nigel turned to looked to the woods to the left of the cliff.  "I think they headed that way, Cara likely thinking they could make it to the trail there.  I looked around.  They were cut off and herded to the edge."

John nodded.  "That's what I'm reading. Sure you don't want to join the force?" He laughed at the look Nigel sent his way.  "Now, what did your friend say about what he found?"

"Other than asking me for a shovel and then sending me for help, not much.  He suspected there's a body under there."

John turned to stare at the cabin remains.  "SueAnn is working there now." He sighed.  "We don't need this right now,

Nigel. Not with the damage and devastation from the tornado. Your family doesn't need this, trying to get back up and running." He pointed to where the stretcher bearing Corin was coming over the edge of the cliff. "And your friend there. How long will he be laid up for?"

Nigel sighed. "I know, John. Listen I'm heading in with Cara. Let Dad know?"

"That's what he said he wanted you to do. Your mom's already there. Your Dad wanted to wait here for now to see what was going on. If Cara hadn't spoken to him, he would have been with you."

"I know." Nigel turned to walk away, before turning back. "Thanks, John. I know your wife will have the prayer chain already going."

"That Belle likely has done. You know her well." John helped shut the rig door behind Nigel and then stepped back to assess Corin.

Corin was still unconscious, an IV line already running to his arm. John spoke for a few minutes with the paramedics before he looked around, beckoning one of the younger officers over. A few quick words and the officer was in the back of the rig with Corin, heading off to the hospital.

Bruce stood beside John, his eyes on the settling dust. "Why, John? What did we ever do to anyone?"

John shrugged. "I have no idea, Bruce. But just remember, God is there in all this. Trust Him."

Bruce snorted, drawing a smile from his cousin. "I know. Trust God. But it's hard when it's your baby girl who was hunted and run down like that. I feel like I'm standing on the edge of that cliff myself, ready to head over." He walked towards the cabins, John at his side. "Now, what about this? What Corin found?"

SueAnn Whyte looked up at his words. "Just getting started, Bruce. John, it's definitely human and from what I've found so far, we seem to have two bodies, an adult and a child. I'm going to suggest we check out the other cabins nearby, just to confirm there aren't any more."

"Any more?" Bruce's voice rose. "You mean, there may be more?" Shock and horror played across his face.

They all turned at a shout from behind them, and then SueAnn was running towards the tech frantically waving at her.

John's heart sank. No, please, Lord. No more. Bruce headed that way, right on John's heels.

Sliding to a stop, SueAnn stared at her tech as he spoke rapidly, his face white with shock, before she turned to the two men, her face grim.

"More bodies, John. Two, Bobby thinks."

"A family." Bruce stared at the cain remains. "Who went missing all those years ago that we never found?"

"No one, Bruce. That's the thing. I've been on the force for years and I don't remember anyone going missing." John sighed. His workload had just increased, and he was down two officers from injuries suffered during rescue attempts from the tornado.

Nigel gripped the bedrail in front of where he sat and leaned his chin on his hands, his eyes on his sister as she picked at the bandage around her wrist and hand, a disgruntled look on her face.

"You can't pull that off, Cara. You know that." He had a grin on his face as he teased her, but concern darkened his amber eyes to almost brown.

She sighed, lifting her arm. "I know I can't, but how long did he say I needed this? I can't be laid up. We have stuff we need to be doing. Camp will open before we're ready for it."

"We'll be ready. The board has already met and assessed what needs to be done. They have indicated there are some small portable cabins that they can bring in if we need to. They'll look at that in about three or four weeks." He sighed as he glanced at the door. "Who did this to you and Corin, Cara?"

She shook her head, her eyes sliding closed against the sudden shaft of pain hitting behind her eyes. She could feel the scratches on her face, but from what Nigel had said, Corin had taken the brunt of the fall, protecting her as much as he could. She hadn't expected that, not after how she had been treating him. Her fingers found the bandage again until a hand stopped hers. She looked up to see her father standing there. Her mother had said she was going to check on Corin and would be back.

"Dad?" She looked up, almost pleading with him. "I want out of here. Can you spring me?"

Bruce shook his head as he grinned at his daughter. She had him wrapped around her little finger but this was one time that wouldn't work. "Not this time, love. You need to stay in overnight. John said he'd have Peter at your door all night."

"A guard? And Peter at that?" Peter was John's son and loved to tease Cara.

"Yes. Peter. Now behave yourself. We'll come get you first thing in the morning." He shared a look with Nigel and knew Nigel wasn't budging from his sister's room.

"Have you had word on Corin?" That wasn't what Nigel wanted to ask, but he didn't want to alarm Cara any more than she had been. Bruce had told him about the second discovery, and his faced had paled at that even as he asked how and who.

"He's still unconscious, from what I understand. They were sending him for some imaging. You know me. I can't keep the alphabet soup of those clear as to which is what."

Cara and Nigel laughed at their father and the comical look on his face before Bruce continued.

"Unfortunately he did break his left arm, likely in the initial fall. Like you, Cara, bumps, bruises, some cuts and scrapes. It's the head they concerned about."

Cara stared at her father. "He can't go home and live on his own, can he? At least not for the first few days. Didn't he say he hadn't unpacked much yet, Nigel?" Bruce and Nigel exchanged grins, that Cara didn't see. She was sounding panicked at the fact his house was in shambles and he wouldn't survive living like that, as she seemed to think.

"Relax, Cara. Mom is taking care of that. She's going to have Corin come stay with us. He's going to working on the cabins, so it makes sense."

She laid back on the pillows, relief coursing through her and over her face. "It does. Dad, are you sure he's okay?"

"No, I'm not, Cara but Mom said she'd be back soon. God was looking after you two today, you know that, don't you?"

She nodded. "I do, Dad. It doesn't make the hurt any easier. I'm going to be dreaming about that fall for months, if not years."

"Maybe. How much do you really remember?" Nigel reached for his sister's hand, his hand warm on her cold one.

"Not a lot. I remember us running towards the woods, getting cut off and then telling Corin not to go that way, but we couldn't get away from them." She looked up, fear lurking in her eyes. "I can remember the ground crumbling under our feet and Corin….." She looked up, shock and surprise on her face. "He saved me, didn't he? He wrapped me in his arms and caught me to him. He took the brunt of it, didn't he?" Tears filled her eyes and spilled over, smarting on the cuts.

Bruce sighed and then reached for his daughter, drawing her tight to him. "That he did, love. He saved you and himself at the same time."

# Chapter 3

*C*orin's head tossed from side to side as he groaned, trying to pry his eyes open, only to clamp them shut against the pain he felt from the light shining in them, dim as it was. He tried once more, this time opening them slowly and only a crack. He looked around, feeling the pull on his arm and seeing the IV lines and then the cast on his left arm. He groaned again. How was he to work with his arm in a cast? He was just trying to get his business going and now this?

A soft hand touched his good hand and he looked up to see Emma Lawson standing here, concern on her face, even as she reached to call for the nurse.

"Corin? You're awake. That's good." Emma's hand reached to push the hair off his forehead, just as she would have for her own son. She considered Corin another son, had done that for years.

"Emma? Where am I?"

"You're in our hospital, Corin. You were hurt. It's been twenty-four hours since you were brought in and this is the first you've really awakened."

He laid his head back and lifted his arm to stare once more at the cast. "What did I go and do, Emma? I don't remember."

The nurse shared a look with Emma and nodded at her, indicating for Emma to continue.

"You fell, Corin. You fell over the cliff near one of the cabins." She stopped, unable to continue for the tears clogging her throat.

"I fell? Over a cliff? That can't be possible. I know better than that." He fastened his eyes on her face, reading something there she hadn't wanted him to. "Wait. Who was with me?"

"Cara was. She went over with you, but you protected her as much as you could. You don't remember what happened yesterday at all?" When he shook his head, she sighed. "Then I guess I have to tell you. You were looking at the demolished cabins and found something in the dirt. Nigel left to call for help and two dirt bikes chased you and Cara, sending you over the cliff." She gripped his hand, her fingers white at the tightness. "You really don't remember, do you? God protected you two. You could have been killed, so very easily and weren't."

Corin sat up, motioning to the nurse. "Pull the IV." When she stared at him, he repeated himself. "Either pull the IV or I will. I'm leaving."

"You can't. You have a concussion and the doctor has to see you. He'll be by in about an hour."

Corin gave her a disgusted look and reaching over, pulled the IV, clamping a hand over the spot to stem the blood. "No, you don't understand. I'm out of here. I need to make sure Cara is okay and doesn't get hurt."

Emma stared at him for a moment before her face softened. He cares about her, doesn't he, Lord? Enough to jeopardize his own health. "Corin, listen to the nurse. She'll bandage that, you can get dressed, but we wait for the doctor to come round. I have to wait for Bruce or Nigel anyway to come for me and they won't be here for a while yet. You'll be staying with us."

He shook his head. "I can't. I have to work."

"You won't be working, not physically for a few days. The police still haven't released the area yet and John says it will be a few more days yet before they do. They've brought in cadaver dogs to search each cabin."

"Cadaver dogs?" Corin's voice held his shock, as the nurse shook her head. She had spoken with Emma briefly about what had been found. Rumours had spread through the town quickly. "Why?"

"Because, what you found were human remains. They found more in the next cabin."

"Bones? I thought that." His head dropped. "I can remember now. Did we really go over the cliff?" He looked up, one eye squinting against the light.

"You did. Now, here's your clothes. We'll leave you to get dressed, but no leaving. Not until the doctor sees you. I'll be standing right outside your door and will see you if you even try."

Corin gave her a quick grin, knowing Emma would do just that.

Cara watched as Corin carefully made his way up the steps into their sprawling one level home, standing back by the kitchen where he couldn't see her. She wasn't ready yet to face him, knowing she would need to apologize for how she had treated him. God had worked on her last night, and she realized she had been jealous of him and his friendship with her brother. She sighed, knowing that it was inevitable that she and Nigel would grow apart now that they were adults.

She turned her head as she felt an arm come around her shoulders. Nigel stood beside her, watching his friend, but keeping a close eye on his sister.

"You okay?"

She nodded. "I think so. I'm worried about him though. He took a beating yesterday."

"He did, but he did it gladly, just to keep you safe. Did you ever think what might have happened if you two hadn't fallen like you did? What would they have done to you?"

She stared at him, horror in her eyes. "Nigel? What aren't you saying?"

"That they would have chased you down and run you down. You wouldn't have walked away from it as well as you did if that had happened."

"Nigel?" She turned into his shoulder and his arms hugged his sister tight, knowing just how close they had come to losing her yesterday.

"You would have more than likely died, Cara, and we don't know who or why. That's the scary part. John will want to talk to you both at some point." He set her back from him, his hands on her shoulders, ducking down so he could see into her eyes. "Do you understand that for some reason you are not safe? That neither one of you are? That's part of the reason Dad wants Corin here. John's asked him to do that. Mom wants him here so she can mother him." He grinned at his mother as she walked by and swatted him on the arm. "Now, come on, let's go see how Corin is."

Corin looked up as the siblings walked towards him, their socked feet quiet on the hardwood floor. He went to stand but stopped when Cara shook her head.

"Don't get up, Corin. You don't have to. How are you feeling?" Cara sat beside her, her hand on his good arm.

"Like I was run over by a truck or dove off a cliff." He grinned at her frown. "Relax, Cara. I'm okay. We survived, didn't we, when we shouldn't have?"

Nigel sat in a rocking chair near them, his toe setting it into motion, his light brown hair reflecting the light from the fire burning in the large rock fireplace. "Now what,

Corin? You're not able to work. I know you've been told not to, not for a week, not with that concussion."

"I know, but we can work on the preliminary plans. Did you happen to grab my laptop?"

Nigel nodded. "I did and I've been told not to let you have it for a couple of days. The doctor wants you to rest your eyes and head, at least until the weekend. You need to."

Corin shook his head and then groaned. "Now, why did I go and do that for? Nigel, we need to get working on the plans. That way, once the land is released again, we can get right to work."

Nigel pointed at Cara. "That's where Cara comes in. You bring up your program for materials and she fills in what you need. Pen and paper, the old-fashioned way, for planning for now. Mom will make sure you rest."

Corin sat back, a black look on his face as Nigel laughed at him. Finally he nodded. "I know what you're saying and why, but we have a time crunch here, Nigel. We need to get working on the buildings to get them up and ready for your camp to open."

Nigel nodded. "We do, but the board has come up with an alternative plan for the summer, depending on how much we can done. They've found some rental cabins that would suit, not the same, but they will do if we have to. They're brought on site and set up for us."

Corin finally agreed. "I can see you're ahead of me on this. Now, what was the plan for the rest of the day, seeing as I'm banned from working?"

Cara stood and then surprised him by grabbing his feet and swinging them up on the couch, causing him to lie down. She reached for the red and black plaid throw on the back of the couch and tucked it around him, her hand resting lightly on his shoulder for a moment. "For now, you rest. Mom will be back with something for you to drink and your pain medications. We'll take this up later."

Nigel tilted his head back to watch her walk away towards the kitchen, and then brought his focus to Corin, a frown crossing his face as he caught the look on his friend's face. He sighed. Lord, why now? Why did Corin suddenly discover he's interested in Cara? This is not a good time, now is it?

"Corin?" Nigel's quiet voice brought his attention back to him. "What's going on?"

Corin stared at him for a moment, then sighed. "What changed with Cara? She doesn't treat me like this."

"No, she doesn't but she just did. Don't hurt her. Treat her with care." Nigel stared at the fingers he was rubbing together, not quite sure how to continue but knowing he had to. "When Cara was in her late teens, she had a boyfriend we all thought was serious about her. Turns out he wasn't as serious as we thought and ended up leaving town with her best friend. We heard later they lived together for a while, had a baby, and then he split from her. She's never come back to town."

Corin stared at Nigel. "He did that to our Cara? Don't let me catch him." Nigel grinned to himself at the vehemence in Corin's voice. "It's no wonder she backs away like she does when I get near her. I wish I had known, Nigel."

"It wouldn't have made any difference, not with Cara. She'd have just kept backing away from anyone who came close to her." Nigel turned his head as he heard a sound and saw his mother approaching. "Mom, where's Cara gotten to?"

"Outside, I think, she said. Something about checking out the shed and the sports equipment." She looked at Nigel as he gave a groan and then rose, heading for his boots and the outside. "What's wrong with him?"

"He doesn't want Cara on her own, not until we find these guys." Corin sat up and took the glass and medication from Emma.

"What did Nigel say to you?" She smiled as his discomfort. "Playing big brother for the first time with you, is he? Don't take it personally. He does it all the time with her. He's been so protective of her, maybe too much so."

"He told me what happened and I get that." He looked down at the glass he still held, his finger rubbing away the condensation on it before he looked up at Emma, almost a pleading look in his eyes. "I won't hurt her, Emma. Not if I can help it."

"We know you won't intentionally, Corin, but she has depths to her where she hides things that not even her family has ever seen. It will take a special person to bring that out. You, I think, are the man God has sent to do just that." Emma stood, then rested her hand on Corin's head as she prayed for him and for her daughter.  She took the glass and walked away, leaving Corin staring at the fire, his hand rubbing his shoulder where Cara's hand had rested without being aware of what he was doing.  He sighed.  Lord, we're in the middle of something, and I decide it's time to get interested in a lady, something I have never done before.

# Chapter 4

Corin watched from his perch on the window sill later that afternoon as the family gathered around John.  He had appeared suddenly at their door, asking to meet with them all.  Corin had tried to leave but John had pointed at him and told him bluntly he was staying, he was the one who started all this and he would stay and see it through to the end.  Corin had stared at him in shock until John had winked at him.

Cara sat beside him, close enough her arm brushed his and he caught the faint smell of coconut from her hair.  She leaned against him, a first for her, and spoke in a low voice.

"What does John want?  Did he say?"

Corin shook his head.  "No, just that he wanted to talk to all of us.  It has to be about those bodies, I would think."

John finally entered the room with Bruce, deep in conversation, a file in his hand.  He looked around, his keen eyes assessing each one of them gathered there before he sat in one of the armchairs and dropped the file onto the side table. He sighed. He was no further ahead, had no idea who the skeletons belonged to. Lord, we need answers and I don't have them.

"John?" Emma spoke, her eyes searching Bruce's face even as she spoke.

"Emma, I can't tell you who they are. I have no idea. We have a man, a woman, a teenager, girl they think, and a child, a boy, they think. SueAnn is still working through that. She's called in a forensics anthropologist to help. And no, we don't know who they are. We haven't had any missing people reports in the area for a family. I'm pulling out the word to surrounding areas, but they could be from a distance."

Bruce nodded. "That I can see. If they had come to camp, then maybe we might have a record of a registration for someone who didn't show, but I can't recall having a family not show."

Emma shook her head. "We never did. If they are a family, that is."

John stared at her, then groaned. "Emma, you just complicated it, you know."

Corin leaned over and spoke low to Cara. "Do you remember anything from that long ago? John thought fifteen years."

"No, but I should have, shouldn't I, if I knew?"

He shrugged. "Not if you didn't think it was important. You might have buried it."

She snorted. "Yeah, I could have done that." She stared at her mother before looking at him. "I vaguely remember rumours among the kids about something from then, but I can't remember what it was."

John was watching them and rising, came to stand beside them, leaning a shoulder on the wall, his hands in his pockets. "Cara? What did you remember?"

"How did you know I did?" She looked up at him, a smile lurking in her eyes.

"I know you. You've remembered something."

She shook her head. "No, not really. It's just there were rumours among the kids, about people that disappeared during a full moon. It was around that time." She thought for a moment. "I can't remember too many of the details. I just shrugged it off as kids' imaginations. Would Peter remember?"

John thought for a moment. "I have no idea. I'll talk to him later. You can't remember anything at all?"

She shook her head once more. "No. If I did know anything, I've buried it too deep. That's not something I even wanted to think about."

"No, that's never been your scene. Can you give me a list of the kids you think might have known something? We can go through your yearbook, but if you can do that, it's a start."

She nodded. "I'll work on it, John. I don't like it though."

John sighed, his eyes catching the look on Corin's face as he watched Cara and wondered. "There are lots of things in life we don't like having to do, Cara, but most times, we don't have a choice." He walked away on those words, leaving her staring after him, Nigel's eyes shifting between Corin and Cara.

"Cara?" Corin's voice was low.

"What?" She snapped at him, then sighed. "I'm sorry, Corin. You didn't deserve that."

"No, I didn't and apology accepted. Now, how be we head to your Dad's office and see what we can accomplish?"

She stared at him. "You just got out of the hospital and you want to work? Not happening. At least not with my help. Not tonight." She stood and stalked away. Corin heard the quiet sound of her door clicking shut and knew she wouldn't be back right away. *Lord, she's hurting and doesn't even know it. Heal her, please. Protect her.*

"What did you say to her?" Nigel's amused voice caught Corin's ear.

Corin eyed his friend, seeing the grin on his face. "Just that I wanted to work, and she refused to help me."

"Can't say as I blame her. You're not supposed to be, you know."

"I know, but I feel so useless right now."

Nigel sat on the wide window ledge beside his friend, his hands jammed into his pockets. He could feel the object he had stuck in there earlier, not sure when he would have an opportunity to talk to Corin.

"You're not useless. You're reaching Cara in a way I've never seen her react to anyone outside the family. Inside the family, for that matter. She watches you to make sure everything is okay with you. That's how Cara is with those she cares about. But it's different with you. Give her time. She'll come around."

He pulled his hand out of his pocket and studied the thumb drive he had had in his pocket. "Corin, I'm going to do something I've never done before and probably shouldn't be doing even now." He reached out his hand, dropping the drive into Corin's. "When you're able to look at a computer screen, study this. It's a video taken years ago of Cara and her friends. See what you think of it and then come talk to me. There's something there I can't put my finger on. I think I'm too close to Cara."

"And I'm not." Corin sounded glum at that.

"It's not that. You weren't around back then." He sighed. "Yeah, it's about fifteen years ago, right around the time those people would have disappeared. I had forgotten the timing of it." He reached for the drive, finding Corin closing his hand and withdrawing it from his reach. "I need to give that to John."

"No, not yet. Let me look at it. I'll make the effort. Then, we'll talk. I have a feeling things are going to go bad for Cara and I would like to prevent that if possible."

"I know you would. You and me both."

Corin rose and walked away, heading for the room they had told him to use. He shut the door quietly, leaning back against it, his eyes raised to the ceiling. Lord, now what? What does Nigel expect me to see that he hasn't?

He moved from the door, taking a look back at it before he reached for his laptop, booting it up and then plugging in the thumb drive. He waited for it to load, his eyes on the screen but not seeing what was there. He finally opened the video and played through it, a frown on his face. He rubbed his eyes, finding it hard to follow the movement. He went back to the beginning and played it again, this time his hand reaching out to stop the video. This is what Nigel was looking for, wasn't it, Lord? He did a screen shot of it and then continued to search.

He finally sat back, his hands reaching to rub at his eyes, and then setting the laptop on the desk in the room. Lord, I know what I've seen but I'm not sure I'm right. Who do I talk to?

He heard a tap at his door and rose, opening it to find Cara standing there, uncertainty on her face.

"Corin? Mom said to tell you supper's almost ready, if you're wanting to eat."

"I do, Cara. Thank you." He reached out and pulled her close, wrapping his arms around her in a hug. He felt her hesitation before she hugged him back, her arms tight around him.

"Thank you, Corin."

"You're welcome, Cara. I'm just glad you weren't hurt."

She stepped back, her eyes on his cast. "But you were and you shouldn't have been. John can't help us. He doesn't have enough information."

Corin sighed to himself, knowing exactly where she was headed with what she was saying. "No, we're not investigating on our own. We have enough to do just getting the camp back together."

"But we can't work on that all the time. You're handicapped right now anyway. Dad says the board wants to wait until the cleanup on Saturday before they make decisions about what to do. We will rebuild. Just not likely where those two cabins were. That's a given."

"That's a shame, knowing how much you like that one area. How close is it to the edge of the property?" Corin turned Cara towards the kitchen, an arm around her shoulders. He felt her lean into him and wondered at that.

"Right on the edge, I think. The property ends at the creek. Why?"

"Who owns the property next to you?"

"Some company or other, I think. It's been vacant for years. Any buildings are falling down." She looked up at him, dawning comprehension on her face. "You don't think?"

He shook his head as they neared the kitchen door, where he could hear the rest of her family moving around. "Not right now. We'll talk later. Tomorrow, we'll do some research."

She nodded and slipped away from his embrace, heading to help her mother with the meal. Bruce shot Corin a look but didn't say anything, content to wait for Corin to approach him.

Two days later, Corin sat back in his chair, his eyes on the paper he had been drawing plans on it. He sighed. It was so much easier doing this in his computer program but he had finally agreed not to use it, having suffered the headaches and blurred vision from trying to follow the flickering images.

Cara stood watching him for a moment, a mug of coffee and plate of cookies in her hands. Her mother was doing her best to make sure Corin ate at regular intervals. She looked down at the food and then turned, thrusting it into her brother's hands and ran from the room. Nigel stared after her for a moment, then brought his eyes to Corin who hadn't moved from where he sat.

Nigel slid the mug and plate in front of Corin, moving his papers aside as he did so.

Corin absentmindedly thanked him, his eyes on the plans, before he picked up the papers and handed them to Nigel.

"These are Cara's dreams, Nigel. I want to incorporate them as much as I can. She's put a lot of thought into them. Did she ever show it to you?"

Nigel shook his head. "No, she never did, and I know for a fact she didn't show

Mom or Dad. Dad would have worked with her on them if she had.”

“Why on earth not?”

Nigel shrugged. “That’s something you’ll have to ask her. I have no idea.” He read through Cara’s notes, seeing the names she had dreamed of for each cabin, with the decor of the cabins going with each name. “She’s good. I like this. She’s wasting her talents just working here.”

“Don’t demean her work here, Nigel. She’s where she feels she’s supposed to be. And I’ve come to know her well enough to know she won’t move on until and unless God tells her to.”

Nigel nodded thoughtfully. “You’re right. You’ve picked up on something we’ve missed. Thank you.” He sat still for a moment, then rose. “I need to find her. She was here and then left.”

Corin rose as well, his hand on Nigel’s arm. “Let me. You’re too close to her.”

Nigel stared after him as he walked away, looking around to find his mother standing there. Emma walked towards Nigel, hugging him before she moved past.

“Mom?”

Nigel's voice stopped Emma and had her turning to look at her son. "What is it, Nigel?"

"Do we take Cara for granted? Do we keep her from moving on and finding her own path in life?"

Emma walked back to her son, her hands coming to rest on his arms. "No, we don't. She and I have had many talks on just this topic. She's where she's content to be for now. She's working through a college course on line. You didn't know that? She's taking designing and home decor. She hasn't said much, but I have no idea what her plans are. I'm not sure she even knows. She said it was just something she felt compelled to do." She shot a look towards where Corin had disappeared. "Maybe, just maybe….." Her voice died away.

Nigel waited for his mother to continue, but when she didn't, he just had to ask. "Mom? What are you thinking?"

"Nothing, Nigel. Absolutely nothing." She linked her arm through her son's and led him away to the kitchen. "I need your help. We have food to prepare for the work bee on Saturday. I know there will be food brought, but you know me."

"That I do, Mom. What first?"

Corin caught up with Cara as she stood at the pasture fence, watching the few animals they kept for camp purposes graze or move around. He stood for a few minutes, watching her face, not quite sure if he should approach her or not, finally choosing to do that. His feet moved him forward without conscious thought, until he stood next to her. He reached to grip the rail of the fence, his fingers going white with the strength of his grip. What he really wanted to do was wrap his arms around Cara and take her away somewhere safe, and that he knew he couldn't do.

"Corin, what are you doing out here?"

"Just standing with a friend, if she'll let me." He held up a hand as she went to protest. "I know. John has asked that you not be on your own. That's not why I'm out here, Cara. I'm out here because you are hurting and you need someone just to stand with you in silence."

She stared at him, not quite sure what to think. "Okay, well, then." Her voice died away. She wasn't quite sure what to make of him. He was so different from what she had thought him.

He grinned at her and then held out his hand. "Truce?"

She shook her head at him even as she reached for his hand. "Truce." She screamed as he suddenly pulled her towards him and then to the ground, his body covering hers as he wrapped his arms around their heads. She struggled to get free, unable to get away from him.

"Corin! What are you doing?"

"Stay still, Cara. Someone's shooting at us."

She froze. "Shooting? At us? How do you know?"

"Because I heard the shot and saw the chips of wood fly from the rail right where you were just standing." He heard shouts as the men ran towards him, some heading towards the trees.

The workers that had been hired to help clean up the mess before the work bee on Saturday reached to help the two to their feet and surrounding them, rushed them to the house. Emma stood just inside the door, her hands to her mouth, wondering what was happening now.

Nigel took one look and was gone, his feet pounding on the ground as he ran after the men heading towards the trees, shouting to his mother to call for John and help. His father was off site, sourcing out material and furnishings they'd need.

Emma wrapped an arm around her daughter and reached for Corin, her hand tight on his as she dragged them to the kitchen and shoved them down into chairs, nodding at one of the workers who held up his phone before disappearing. She knew some of the men would stay around the house, just to keep them safe.

Cara brushed at the tears on her face. "Thank you, Corin. I..I..I'm sorry. I just seem to bringing trouble to you."

Corin reached over to trace a finger through the tears, then used his thumbs to wipe them away. "Not you, Cara-mine. Not you. It's whoever did the deed fifteen years ago. We just got involved because we found the evidence."

She stared at him even as she nodded, liking the feel of his hands of her face, before frowning. What had he just called her? And did he even realize that? She took the cup of peppermint tea her mother handed her, her fingers curling into the warmth of the cup.

Corin sat back, his thoughts black at whoever it was. This was the second time they had almost killed Cara.  Who was it? And why?  He was no closer to knowing, not yet anyway.  He had put in a call to a friend, asking him to research the property next to him.  He knew Levi Blackwell or Blackie as he was known would find out everything he could or else his father would.

"Corin?  What happened out there?" Emma's voice broke through his thoughts.

"Someone took a shot at Cara."  He watched as Emma paled, her face as white as Cara's.

"You're sure it was Cara they were after?"

"It has to be.  She was with me, was it only a few days ago, when we found the skeletons.  Everyone knows that's her favourite cabin, don't they?  I suspect someone has been watching it since the tornado went through, to see if she came around and found what we found."

"But I didn't find it!"  Cara's protest broke out.  "You did."

"I know.  That's beside the point. You were there.  They know you know the area and knew just where to chase you to, to harm you."  He watched as she paled further, her mother reaching to clasp her hand.  "I don't, so I would have had no idea where to run. You did.  Cutting us off like they did make sure we had to go over the cliff.  If I had been on my own, I would have stood and fought them.  I couldn't with you there and they knew that."  He paused, a horrible thought crossing his mind.  No, he thought, that can't be.

"Corin?"  Cara's puzzled voice brought his head up.

He shook it, not willing to say anything yet.  "You're okay, Cara?  I didn't hurt you?"

"No, just scared me.  I didn't know what you were doing.  I didn't hear anything."  She looked at her mother, horror on her face.  "The animals."

"The men will look after them.  Nigel's out there as well."  Emma stood, her hand resting on her daughter's head as she prayed for the two.  Lord, I have no idea it would be this severe.  We certainly need your protection.

Corin raised his head again as he heard Nigel's voice as he headed for the kitchen. He caught the fear on Cara's face before she schooled her features and hid it.  He stopped as he went to speak, knowing that this was what she did all the time.  Hid her emotions so she didn't upset anyone.  What drove her to do that, Lord?  Was she always like that?  Somehow, I think whatever happened with her boyfriend is what did it.

Nigel slid into a chair, a mug of coffee in front of him.  John stood, leaning against the counter, one hand bracing himself there, the other holding the mug he had been handed.  He sipped at his tea, his eyes on Corin and then Cara.  He sighed to himself.  Why now, Lord?  Who is it?

"Any closer to finding the identities?"  Emma watched her daughter closely as she asked that.

John shook his head.  "Not really.  We have some possibilities but nothing concrete.  Not yet.  It's going to take time, given it's been so long."

Cara shared a look with Corin, then spoke.  "That property's been left alone for so long, John.  Any possibility they were connected with it and not us or the camp?  It would have been pretty convenient to kill them and then bury them under the cabins.  I've done some research.  That property belongs to a numbered company.  Corin verified that."

John stared at them, the possibility of them finding something else that would put them into further danger raising in his mind, but he knew Cara. He knew that no matter how often or how firm his voice when he told her to stay out of the investigation, she wouldn't. Not when it involved her family and friends. He watched the glances and interactions between the two and realized something more was going on. Just great, he thought, then asked the Lord for forgiveness. It was about His timing, not theirs, he thought.

"We've thought of that but haven't gotten enough information to go any further yet. We can't just be walking in blind to that, Cara. We need to know there's a reason to look into that."

She opened her mouth to protest but felt Corin's hand gently squeeze hers and her mouth snapped shut, before she reluctantly nodded. "I understand, John. I had done some research on it a while ago, just from curiosity. Corin has helped me in the last couple of days." Her head went down on her folded arms, fatigue suddenly claiming her as the adrenaline released.

Nigel gave a sound, then stood, gathering Cara into his arms and heading for her bedroom, tucking her into bed before closing her curtains and standing for a moment watching her sleep. This was not her, he thought, but she's been through a lot in the last few days. She hasn't taken the time she needed to recover from the fall, pushing herself to work and keep going. He gently closed the door behind him, finding Corin standing just away from it in the hall.

"Nigel?"

Nigel sighed. "She's okay, Corin. She just needs some sleep. She hasn't stopped since she came home from the hospital. I've heard her pacing at night. That's not her."

"No, it's not." Corin shot a glance at the door and then back down the hall. "Can we go somewhere we can talk, where we won't be overheard?"

"Yeah, I guess. If you think it's important." Nigel held up his hands. "Forget I said that. I know you. It's important. Come on. The attic room will work."

"That it will." Corin followed Nigel up the stairs to the attic and stood staring around. "I like this space. This would make a nice apartment, you know."

"And who would it be for? Besides, Mom and Dad will never do that."

"I know." Corin paced, not quite sure how to proceed.

Nigel watched him, finally speaking. "Something's on your mind. Spit it out."

Corin shook his head even as he grinned at his friend. "It's about what going on. I had a horrible thought. What if it was Cara's friend, the one who left? Would he have been involved in something like this? I'm not sure when he left, if he was even still around at that point."

Nigel stared at Corin, his face blank, but his mind racing. He thought long and hard before he spoke, his words soft. "He was. Yes, I could see him being involved in something like this. He would know the area and know how Cara loves that particular spot." He sighed, spinning and pacing, his hands pushing through his hair. "This may be the answer who went after you two, but it wouldn't explain the bodies."

"No, it wouldn't. Tell me about him. What all was he involved in that you know about but that Cara won't?"

Nigel stood at the window, a hand resting on the wall on either side of it, his chin falling to his chest. He drew a deep breath. Lord, this has just gotten so much worse. Why? Why does Cara have to go through the pain all over again? And if Corin's right, she will.  She 's going to need You like she never has before.

"There were rumours about him, Corin, rumours that we could never prove.  Trust me, Dad and I tried as did John.  He was too clever.  It was said he was involved in drugs, in protection, in break and enters, identity theft."  He spun, his eyes hardening.  "That could be why we can't find out who these people are.  If he was involved and sold their identity on the black market, it would appear these people are still alive."

"That's a good point, Nigel."  John stood in the doorway before he entered and closed the door.  "Sorry, I don't mean to interrupt a private conversation but I figured you two had headed up here when you disappeared."

"That's not a problem, John, not on my part."  Nigel threw a look at Corin and caught him shaking his head as well.  "What was it you wanted from us?"

John studied the two younger men, knowing they were both determined to protect Cara, each with their own reasons for doing so, even to the point they would give their lives for her.  "Someone has to stay with Cara at all times.  She can't be wandering around on her own.  That's what she did today. If you hadn't been there, Corin, she would have been seriously injured or more likely killed."

Corin paled. "It was that close?"

John nodded. "We checked. Where she was standing when she reached for you and moved towards you? That's exactly where the bullet hit. It would have likely hit her in the chest."

Nigel slumped back against the wall. "It was that close?"

"It was, Nigel. Now do you two understand how serious this is? I know you did before, but we need to get that through to Cara. She's not listening to me. If these attacks continue, I'll put her into custody of some kind and lock her away. And you both know how well that will go over."

Nigel nodded. "We'll stay with her, or keep her in the house. No. That won't work. She'll never go for that." He looked at his friend. "Corin. Any suggestions?"

Corin started to laugh. "You know her better than I do. Why would I have any suggestions?"

"Because she's doing what you say, not what we are asking her to. She's listening to you, not us."

John's eyes flew between the young men, picking up on what Nigel was implying. He wasn't the only one who had seen that, then, he thought, and sighed once more.

Corin shook his head. "No, she won't listen to me either."

John held up his hands. "It doesn't matter who she listens to, as long as she does what I'm asking. There will be a lot of activity around here in the next few weeks, a perfect time for someone to come after her. Peter has said he'll help out as much as he can. He's already planning on taking a leave to come work here. I'm letting him, putting him on duty here."

"You don't have the men to do that, John."

"I can and I will. The men and women on the force have come to me. They want to help in any way they can. I don't think you realize, Nigel, just how far a reach your parents have had in the community. They have touched every single family at some point. Those families are determined to help you get back on your feet, and to keep Cara safe."

"But they have their own work and lives to rebuild."

John nodded. "They know that. This is what a small community does. I don't think you've ever experienced it, not like this." He turned for the door as he finished. "Just keep her safe. That's all I ask. She'll fight me if I have to put her into protective custody and then she'll run and hide. We can't protect her if we don't know where she is."

Nigel stared after John as he walked down the stairs before his gaze turned to Corin, to find him watching him.

"Well, who gets to break the news to her?" Corin grinned at the frown on Nigel's face. "I think it should be you."

"No, I think you should."

"Who should tell who what?" Cara's voice at the door caused the two men to jump and look guilty, causing her to frown as she faced them.

Nigel waved his hand at Corin. "He'll explain. I'm needed somewhere, I'm just not sure where that somewhere is."

Cara stared after him, her mouth open. Corin quickly covered his grin as she turned, frowning at him. "Corin? Care to explain? By the way, Mom has some food ready. But I'm not letting you by me until you tell me."

"Tell you what? That you're very beautiful? That I would like to get to know you better? That John has asked us to keep you safe?" He grinned as her frown deepened and he walked towards her, dropping a kiss on her forehead as he passed her and headed down the stairs.

Cara stared after him before she realized what all he had said. His first words had taken her breath away, making her feel something she hadn't in years. Then, with a frustrated cry, she ran down the stairs after him. "Corin! What did you just say?"

"Which part?" He grinned at her again as he filled a plate with sandwiches and veggies.

"Corin! You know exactly what part. That John wants you to keep me safe!" She was almost in tears, the frustration and fear gaining an upper hand.

He set his plate down and came around the table to stand in front of her before he reached and pulled her to him. "It's okay to be afraid, Cara. I must say that I am. John has asked that we stay with you. He's threatened to pull rank and put you into protective custody. I don't think you'd like that at all."

He felt her tears on his shirt as they started and he wrapped his arms around her. "We want to keep you safe, not destroy you. We don't want you harmed, not any more than you have been." He finally felt her push against him and moved so she could step back. He watched as she swiped at the tears, not looking at him.

"Thank you, Corin. I'll try but I can't live like this forever. You know I can't."

"We don't expect you to." His eyes raised to where he had heard steps and saw Bruce watching his daughter before he glanced at Corin. Corin nodded towards Cara, moving to pick up his plate of food and leaving, just stopping long enough to have a quiet word with Bruce.

Cara turned as she heard him walking away, her eyes finding her father and seeing for the first time the fear for her in his eyes before he shuttered them. "Dad?"

"I just heard, Cara." He swept his daughter into a hug, then set her back, his hands on her arms. "You're okay? Nigel said Corin saved you."

She nodded. "He did. I didn't hear anything and couldn't figure out why he had taken me down." She fought against more tears. "He said John wants to put me into protective custody."

"Only if he has to. So far, that doesn't look as if it's necessary. But promise me something, please? Promise me you'll stay with myself, Nigel or Corin? Don't wander away on your own. If you need some space, let us know. We'll bring you back here so you can have that." His arm came around her and he led her back to the attic. "Your Mom and I have been talking. Make this your studio or office or whatever you want to make it. It's your space now, Cara. Let me know what you need and I'll get it for you."

"You can't, Dad, not right now. Not with the expense for the camp."

He laughed as he stood, staring around the space, trying to imagine how Cara would furnish it. "That's been taken care of. Between the insurance, free labour, and the multitude of donations I was offered, we'll be up and running by the time we need to open. Your young man will have his work cut out for him, broken arm and all, just trying to keep up with everyone. Nigel will work with him. I'd like it if you'd work with him on the interiors of the cabins. I didn't know that you had wanted to do that. You should have talked to me, Cara. I would have told you to do ahead." He headed for the stairs, his voice floating behind him. "I like the idea of naming the cabins instead of just being numbered. Let me see your list and your Mom and I will talk it over with you."

Cara stood, her hands to her mouth in surprise. She had not expected that, not a bit. Her eyes narrowed. Now who had squealed on her, she wondered? It was likely Corin. Nigel wouldn't have said anything, not unless their father had seen her work with Corin and asked him about it.

She spun to take in the room. She had dreamed of just what her father had offered her but never that she would have it for real. She didn't see Corin at first, standing at the top of the stairs, a shoulder propped against the door frame, his broken arm resting on his good arm, one foot crossed over the other. She finally saw him, and stopped, seeing a look on his face she didn't understand, and then approaching him.

"Corin, did you tell?"

"Tell what, love?"

"Tell Dad what I wanted to do?"

He shook his head. "Not a word. He hasn't even seen the plans we've been drawing up. He said he would look at them tonight. Now, your mother. She's been around when we've been talking. She might have seen or heard something. Would she have talked to your father?"

Cara nodded. "That she would have." She sighed, then, a dark look crossing her face. "Corin, I want this over. Dad's told me to fix up this area, that he'll foot the bill for me. I don't know though. There's so much to do."

"How be we take one day at a time? I'll get Nigel to help me move up a couple of the folding tables, some chairs, our computers and printers and a filing cabinet for you and we'll be set to work." He moved into the area. "That is, if that is okay with you. That way, you'll be able to lay out your plans and not have to keep putting them away every night."

She came up beside him and reaching out, hugged him. It surprised him, that she did on her own initiative. But he welcome the warmth she was starting to share, how she was opening up. It's time, isn't it, Lord, time for her to show the world who she really is.

*Chapter 5*

*C*ara blew out a frustrated breath. John had been by and said they were no further ahead in finding the men responsible. He had refused to talk to her about the investigation, telling her it was still in the preliminary stages and he wasn't ready to share just yet.

She paced the attic space, her thoughts not on the plans she was to be working on, missing Corin being there with her. She was coming to rely on him in a way she didn't anyone else, and that scared her. She heard a sound and saw Nigel at the door, a bottle of water held out for her. She had opened the windows to let the breeze flow through, but it was still a warm day.

"Nigel? What isn't John saying?"

He shrugged as he stood in front of one of the tables, his finger idling tracing one of the cabin interiors she was working on. "I like this, Cara. You've really brought out what this camp is all about. What did you name this one?"

"That one? I think it's Peace?"

"That's what it says in what you're doing. Thank you." He reached to hug her and drop a kiss on her head. "Now, what was it you were saying about John?"

"He won't share what he knows, just that he isn't ready yet. How long do I have to feel like a prisoner?" She knew she was pouting and didn't care.

Nigel grinned at the tone of her voice. Yep, Cara was getting ready to break loose and they couldn't have that. "He's likely still pulling in all the information he can. He did say he didn't have confirmation on the identities but he had had some response to his inquiries, and he was sending someone to go talk to that department." He turned so he could rest one hip on the table, idly swinging that leg. "How be Corin or I spring you for a day away?"

"Can we really do that?" Her face lit up at the thought. "Nigel, I so need to get away. I've going crazy being kept around like this. You know how much I hate this."

Nigel's eyes raised to where Corin stood in the doorway. "Then, plan something with Corin and we'll make it happen." He rose, hugging her once more before he walked by, his hand resting on his friend's shoulder for a moment.

"Cara?"

Corin's voice had her spinning around, her hand to her throat. "Corin! I didn't know you were there!"

"I just got here, and heard Nigel saying something about springing you free for a day." He grinned at her look. "So, can you make it tomorrow? If we do something spur of the moment, they might not be able to track us."

"I can, I think. The plans are at a stage where we need to make decisions and I would rather sit on that for a day or two." She walked towards him. "Where could we go where we'd be safe?"

He shrugged. "I don't think it really matters, but there is a little town about a hundred miles from here I'd like to check out. A friend is living there now and has asked me to come visit."

"And what town would that be?"

"Mistletoe. Have you ever been there?"

She stared at him. "Mistletoe? You have a friend there? And no, I have never been. I have always wanted to go. I hear the Christmas celebrations are quite the thing.

But it's only May.  I guess that won't be happening."

"Not Christmas, but they do have celebrations for every season and holiday. Let's plan on running away early tomorrow, before it's really light.  I hear the cafe is quite the place to be seen."

She shook her head at him before turning back to her work, losing the train of thought that had been niggling at her.  Corin watched her, his heart in his eyes, knowing she wouldn't turn around and praying he could recover before she did.  He moved to stand beside her, deliberately in her way, but she didn't look up.

Cara finally handed Corin a plan. "What do you think about this for the cabin we've named Joy?"

He paused at the name, one of which she had chosen and refused to back down from.  He looked at the light bright colouring she had chosen and realized just how talented she was.  God had created something in her that just had to come out.

"This is beautiful, Cara."  He paused, a thought touching him.  "You're working on courses for this, aren't you?"

She turned, surprise on her face. "Who told you?"

He looked down at her, seeing something lurking on her face, a hesitation he wasn't used to seeing. "No one. I just know you are. You're good at this. In fact, we should form a partnership."

"A partnership?" Her voice rose and ended in a squeak. She stared at him, her mouth wide open, not sure what he meant.

Corin looked away before looking back at her, a smirk on his face, a glint of mischief in his eyes, knowing exactly what she was thinking. "Yes. A partnership. You and I working together to build and decorate homes. There's a need here in town. Pray about it, Cara. I have been."

She finally nodded, not quite sure if that was all he meant, but taking the opportunity he was offering her.

The next morning, Cara yawned as she settled back in the truck seat, watching carefully as Corin worked to shift gears, given the cast on his arm making holding the steering wheel difficult. She wasn't quite prepared to spend the day with him, given what they had been through, but God had been working in her heart, asking her to trust Him more fully in all areas.

Corin watched the traffic around him closely, although that early in the morning, there wasn't a lot. He didn't see anything that stood out, but then, he really had no idea of what he would be looking for.

Later that afternoon, Cara sat back once more in the truck, her face flushed with happiness and laughter. Corin shot her a look and was satisfied. It had done her good to get away, to get her perspective back.

Corin had had a text message from Nigel, asking that they be back by suppertime. John was wanting to talk to them both. He didn't like the sounds of that, not at all. He wondered what it was about, and did some heavy praying, knowing it was likely to be a game-changer for them. He hated to ruin the day Cara had just had, but at least they had one day together, away from everything. He would treasure that.

Cara looked up at him as he stood waiting for her walk into the house. She frowned as she saw the look on his face.

"Corin? What's going on? You've been quiet on the way home?"

He reached to trace a finger down her cheek, letting his hand rest on her shoulder. "There is. John's here. He wants to talk to us. Nigel let me know about an hour ago."

"Just before we left to come home? Oh, I'm so glad he waited until then. It would have ruined a perfect day." She turned and slipped away from him, intent on changing into something more comfortable.

He stared after her, shocked at her words, before he felt a hand on his own shoulder and heard Bruce's voice in his ear.

"It looks as if it worked. Thank you for caring so much about our girl, Corin. We didn't worry. We knew she was in good hands and always will be with you."

Bruce opened the door and walked through, leaving Corin to stumble after him, not quite sure of what Bruce had meant. He too headed for his own room, needing a few moments on his own before he faced everyone else.

John looked around at the group gathered at the supper table. They were finished eating and were quietly chatting, the two younger men teasing Cara, who was protesting whatever it was. John smiled. It was so typical of a meal here, that he hated to be the one to break it up.  Bruce caught his eye and nodded, speaking through the voices.

"We need to spend some time in prayer, I think.  John is here to update us, but we need to bring whatever it is to God first and foremost.  Nigel, you lead out."

Finally, Bruce brought their time of petition to a close before rising and topping up their teas or coffees, then turning to John.

"John, as much as we like your company and as much as you're always welcome here at any time, this time it's business.  You have the floor."

John sighed, his eyes searching each face staring back at him, not liking what he was going to have to say, and knowing that Cara and Corin would be the most affected by it.

"I know, Bruce, but thank you, Emma, for the meal.  Delicious, as always.  Cara, Corin.  What I am about to say goes no further.  You are being told where we are in the investigation so that you can take as many precautions as you need to and stay safe.  Even then, we can't guarantee that the people responsible won't get to you in some way.  There are going to be a lot of extra people around over the next few weeks. We are trying to limit them to town people, but there will be occasions when outsiders will be around. During those times, Cara, I would ask that you stay as close to one of the men in your family or to one of my officers as you can. Peter will be around at those times and his only duty then will be you."

"But why me, John?" Cara was puzzled, that he could see.

"Because whoever it has decided to target you. We have an idea who it is but I can't or won't deny or confirm who that is. Corin has been targeted because he happened to be the one who found the bones. From what we can determine, the bodies were buried there fifteen years ago. About the time you had to repair those floors, Bruce, floors you couldn't figure out how they got damaged. I remember discussing that with you at that time. We didn't pull them up, I know, because we didn't see a need to. In hind sight, I guess we should have and we wouldn't be having this conversation.

"Cara, we have reason to believe you have become a target, not just because of this, but for some other reason. And the only reason we can come up with is your old boyfriend."

She paled at that, her hands reaching out blindly to grab at Corin's. "Him? After all these years?  But why?  He told me to get lost and then walked out of my life and our town."

John nodded.  "I know he did, but his family is still here.  There have been rumours, carefully kept from you, that he has been back and forth into town over the years.

"That leads me to the question you two brought up about the property next to you.  As you suspected, it belongs to a numbered company and we're working on determining the actual owners of it.  But it appears as if the people whose bodies we found are somehow connected to it.  We're still working through confirmation of their identities.

"You two are not safe, not yet, not by a long shot.  We have no idea, yet, as to why they decided after all this time you were a threat, Cara.  You must have seen or heard something in the past that at this time brings you into their line of sight.  I don't like that.  Without knowing who or why, our hands are tied."

Cara nodded, her face pale.  "I have no idea, John.  I still have my journals from back then.  I'll go over them but I don't remember anything standing out that would alarm me."  She sighed.  "How long?"

John gave a short laugh. "Your guess is as good as mine, Cara. That is something we have no idea to gauge."

Questions followed, answers to many John didn't have or wouldn't share. He finally rose, leaving the family staring at one another, wondering when it would all end.

Cara was quiet as she rose, helping to clear the table before she excused herself. Nigel stared after his sister, made a move to follow her but stopped when his mother laid a hand on his arm.

"Let her have some time, Nigel. She's been through a lot and there is not end. The most we can do right now is pray for her and for Corin."

Nigel dropped a kiss on his mother's cheek. "I know, Mom, but I still want to do something. Find whoever this is."

"Let John and his people work on that, son." Bruce spoke up from where he was washing the pots. "She'll need our prayers now like she never has before."

Nigel finally nodded, looking around the kitchen. At some point, Corin had slipped away. He needed time by himself and then he wanted to find Cara.

Cara stood at the window overlooking the front of the house, her arms folded around herself, shock coursing through her, but fear as well. She was desperately praying for protection and peace but it wasn't coming, trying hard to keep the tears that wanted to fall locked insider her. She faintly heard feet on the stairs and prayed that her family would stay away. Arms surrounded her and she felt the cast, knowing Corin had come to find her. She leaned back against him, and his chin rested on the top of her head.

"Corin, what are we to do?" Tears were near the surface, tears she absolutely refused to shed.

"We trust God. We trust John. We go on about our daily lives. You stay close to me and I stay close to you." She felt his smile against her hair. "You know, people are going to be talking about us."

She sighed. "I know. They'll think we've become a couple. What are we to do?"

"Become that couple." His arms tightened as she moved. "Listen, just for a moment. I want to ask you something, and then ask you to pray about it." He waited until he felt her nod. "Okay. So we have to stick close to one another, just for our own safety. Would you consider being my girl just for the duration, until we find out who this is and get it resolved?  As you said, people will talk anyway.  This way, it won't seem odd if we're together, even when we're not working.  Your parents and brother would agree.  John would likely think it a wonderful idea.  And who knows, maybe it would end it sooner than later.  He or she seems to have focused on you."

She stilled, her thoughts running rampant.  "Do you really mean that, Corin?  You would take that much of a risk?"  She struggled with him until he let her turn and face him, her head tilted back to look up at him.  "It would be so dangerous for you."

"No more than for you, I suspect.  Just think about it, that's all I ask."

She frowned, picking up on another sentence he had spoke.  "Why are you so sure it's not just a man?"

He shrugged.  "Just putting that out there, I guess.  I know God is in control and knows exactly who it is.  We have to trust Him, Cara, and that's so difficult."

She leant her head on his chest.  "I know.  That scares me you know. The unkown.  The leap of faith.  I feel like we're still on that cliff, just before we went over."  She looked back up.  "Okay, a couple it is for now.  Once whoever it is has been found, we go back to just friends.”

Corin grinned at her.  “Sure. Whatever.”  He knew in his heart she would never just be a friend again.  That was a given.  She had become too much to him, and he feared losing her.

*Chapter 6*

Corin looked up from the wood trim he had been cutting and searched for Cara. He couldn't see her and had a bad feeling she had decided to leave without telling him. He dropped the wood and headed out of the cabin, the one she had named "Serenity". He shook his head. He had no idea what name she was going to up with next.

He found her, sitting on the front steps, leaning back on her elbows, her face raised to the warming sun. He dropped down beside her, content at the moment, for a moment forgetting what they were going through.

"Corin? Why did you chose to come here, to Hollytown?"

He shrugged. "Nigel always spoke so highly of his town. Mom and Dad are travelling so much, there wasn't much to keep me in my hometown. They understood. They can come see me here just as easily as there. I'll likely see more of them."

"But that's not the real reason, is it?" She tilted her head, reaching to brush her hair from her face.

His fingers itched to do just that, but he shook his head instead. "No, it wasn't. Something about this town has drawn me. There's a mission field here, Cara, which your family has tapped into. But there's so much more out there. I have dreams that I haven't told anyone yet." He looked down at her, seeing her eyes still on him. He sighed to himself. How did he continue without spilling his guts over how he felt about her? "You were part of the reason, as well."

She stared at him, a soft sound coming from her. "Then, your request for us to be a couple meant more than just for the duration of whatever we're going through? Is that what you're saying?" She watching him fighting a battle within himself, a battle he finally lost as he nodded, his eyes not leaving her face. She smiled. "Thank you, Corin. You have made me feel something I have not felt in years." She reached out and hugged his arm, her head on his shoulders. Her next words were low enough that he barely heard them, but they gave him hope. "I wouldn't object to that at all."

They sat for a while, the warmth of the spring day beating down on them, silent except for the birds and the insects surrounding them, content just to be with one another and their awakening awareness of one another.

Cara finally broke the silence. "How much more do we have to do on this cabin?"

"Not a lot. I'll have the trim done today. Then, it's just waiting for the painters to move in. You've finished the selection of colours?"

"That I have. I have left the list on the kitchen counter for them and also talked to Paul about it. He's quite happy with the extra work."

"I'm sure he is. He had a rough winter, being sick like he was."

She nodded, her thoughts straying to the other cabins. "How many is it that we've worked on now?"

"Four. We're still waiting on clearance to start the last two. John thought he'd be able to release them within the week. That's good. Thankfully, we don't have to rebuild them all." He frowned as he saw a paper floating near the woods. He wasn't aware that he had lost anything. "Did you drop any papers, Cara?"

She shook her head. "No. Why?"

"Because there's one over there by the trees." He looked around. "This is what I want you to do. Lock yourself in my truck. Please. I'm going to go over and get that paper, but not until you're safe. Please, Cara."

She finally nodded and rose, heading for his truck. He watched as she climbed in and locked the doors, her eyes on him. He headed for the paper, his eyes alert, listening for any sound that should not be there. He reached for the paper, picking it up, his brow darkening as he read it and then folded it away in a pocket. It looked as if he was done work for the day.

Cara watched as Corin headed into the cabin and returned shortly, storing his tools in his truck, then locking the cabin door. He stood for a moment on the steps, looking around, before he headed for the truck and waited until she unlocked the doors before he slid behind the wheel and headed for town.

"Corin? What was on that paper?" She paled at the grim look on his face. "What did it say?"

"That whoever it was is watching you, and that you won't get off so lucky next time." Lord, he prayed, how do I keep her safe?  This is a situation totally out of my control and I don't like it.

"No!  They're following us around, aren't they?"  She twisted in her seat, her eyes searching the surrounding area.  She stilled as his hand came down on hers.

"We're okay so far, Cara.  We need to go find John.  Is he working today?"

She shrugged.  "I have no idea.  He should be, but they were talking of going away for a long weekend, so I don't know for sure."

Corin pulled into a parking spot in front of the police station, his hand holding Cara in place.  "Wait for me to come around, okay?"  He waited for her to nod, then slid out of the truck, rounding the front and opening her door, her hand clasping tight to his.

The desk officer looked up and greeted them, nodding that John was there and he would let him know.

John stood for a moment, his eyes taking in the picture the younger couple made, shaking his head knowing that something had changed for them.

Corin looked up as he heard John approaching them.  "Is there somewhere we can talk, John?"

John nodded, handing them visitors' badges, and leading them back to his office, pointing them to chairs and then perching on the edge of the desk.

"I'm guessing this isn't a social call."

"It's not. I found this. At Serenity Cabin."

"Not so much serenity there, I gather." John carefully took the piece of paper, knowing that there would be no chance of any prints on it. He read it, his face darkening.

"They've been following us, John. That's how they knew where we were. We've been moving to a different cabin each day and we don't know until the morning which one is far enough ahead for us to work on."

John nodded. "That has to be it. That means they're watching your place closer than we thought. Now, what to do about this?" He tapped the paper, his eyes on the floor as he thought through the possibilities and the implications.

"I'm not going into hiding, if that's what you're thinking, John. I absolutely refuse to do that."

"I'm not asking yet, Cara. Did you get a chance to look through your journals?"

She nodded. "I did, and I didn't note anything out of the ordinary that I noticed or heard." She looked at Corin and then back at John. "What do they think I know?"

"That we don't know, yet. We're expecting final confirmation on the names in the next day or so. I'll be out to talk to your folks then. From what we have determined, your camp wasn't involved, other than being the burial spot for them."

She sighed. "Well, there's that, then. Corin, do you have anything else to ask?"

Corin choked back a laugh even as John grinned at her. "Doing John's work for him now, are we, Cara?" He shifted in his chair to miss the playful blow she directed at him. "No, I don't. Not at the moment. Let's get you home and back to work on your cabins." He held up a hand. "No, not the actual cabins. We're done that for the day."

"Give me a call in the morning and let me know which one you'll be working on. I'll have some officers clear the area around it and leave one of them with you for the day." He shook his head at her protest. "Cara, it's what we do. Now, let us do our job."

Cara paced the living room, a frown on her face. Her mother watched her for a while before stepping into her path and causing her to stop.

"Cara, what is it? You've been on edge now since you got home. I don't think it's all to do with the paper Corin found."

Cara sighed, knowing she was going to have to talk with someone and it might as well be her mother.

"Can we talk, Mom? Really talk?"

Emma nodded. "How about over some tea? I think we're going to need it."

Emma watched as Cara played with the string on her teabag, finally reaching over and taking it from her.

"Cara? You wanted to talk. Now, tell me what's going on."

Cara sighed, not quite sure how to go about asking what she needed to ask. "Corin asked me to pretend to be a couple, to throw off whoever it is and make it less obvious that he was protecting me." She paused, her finger flicking at a catch in the tablecloth before her mother's hand covered hers.

"Cara? What's really going on? Are you that upset that he asked you to put up a pretence?"

Cara shook her head. "It's not that, Mom." She raised her eyes finally, looking at her mother, her heart in her eyes, not aware that it was. Emma's heart sank for a moment, not sure what was going on. "Today, he asked if we could make it real. That he wants us to be a couple, not just pretend. That I was one of the reasons he moved here." Tears shimmered in her eyes as her mother reached to draw her into an embrace, her heart praying hard for her girl, but praising God that someone had at least seen the worth of a young lady named Caralee.

"And you're not sure what you want? You're not sure if he's serious. Is that what's been wrong?" Emma's eyes lifted to where Bruce stood, compassion on his face. Bruce leaned against the door frame, not willing to leave, but not willing to let Cara know he was there, not quite yet.

"I know what I want, Mom, but what if he decides he doesn't want me?" Tears wet Emma's sweater.

"Oh, honey. I've seen how he watches you. I don't think that's a concern." Emma's own tears wet her daughter's hair. "You know, we've prayed for a mate for you. Corin fits you exactly." She felt Bruce's arms surrounding them both and then his deep voice offering up a prayer for both Cara and Corin.

Bruce knew that the stress of what the two were facing could very well drive them apart, but it would also drive them closer together. That was how life worked, he thought.

Cara finally sat back, her father's arm still around her as he crouched beside her. She wiped at the tears on her face, not looking at either of her parents.

"Cara, we've been remiss with you. We've been praying for you, but I don't think we've told you how proud we are of you. You are a beautiful young woman, inside and out. Your love of God and family have made you a treasure in our family and in our church. I'm told all the time about things you have done. Things that you have asked not be noised about." She had turned to watch her father, seeing the distress on his face. "From now on, we're making a pact, the three of us that we go forward from this point to tell each other one thing every day what we see about them that we like or want to see in our own lives. You've grown so much over the last few years, but you've kept so much hidden."

He paused, knowing his next words would send her into mixed emotions again.

"Corin sees you even better than we do. He's not as close, not as close as I know he would like to be. He cherishes you already, love, trying to make sure you're taken care of. If he has asked you to consider the next step, then please do. He hasn't asked that lightly or without a lot of prayer. That's who he is."

Cara finally nodded, wiping once more at her face, moving to hug her parents before she rose and walked from the room. Her father claimed her chair, his hands reaching for Emma's.

"Where did we go wrong, Emma?"

She shook her head. "We didn't, Bruce. She's hidden it too well. You can blame Tam for that. He did a number on her as they say."

"He did. I never would have expected it from him, but from what I heard afterwards, Cara was fortunate he left when he did. He left a pretty ugly picture behind him."

Emma saw the dark anger on his face and shuddered. "Then I'm so glad he left. We don't need him anyway." She paused, a thought coming to her. "Do you suppose he's come back or that Beth has returned and they're behind this?"

Bruce shrugged. "It's a possibility I know that John has considered and is investigating. It wasn't common knowledge that his father was part of the company that owned the property next to us. I haven't heard if he sold it off or not. John's aware of that as well."

Emma sighed. "He just can't stay out of her life, can he? I really hope Corin makes that much of a difference in her. I can see it already."

# Chapter 7

Turning slightly as he worked, Corin watched for Cara, not seeing her at first. He moved further from where he stood and watched as she laughed with one of the off-duty paramedics she had been to school with, their teasing of each other wafting across the breeze to him. He smiled, content that she was happy and near him. He returned to his work, whistling under his breath, not paying much attention to the activity around him, other than to listen for Cara.

He heard a soft moan a while later and spun, not seeing where it was coming from. He moved quickly towards the cabin, his feet suddenly propelling him forward. His heart dropped as he ran for the porch, watching Cara.

Cara stood, her hand on the door, her body shuddering, unable to move. Corin ran faster, hitting the porch, yelling for someone to cut the power to the cabin. He heard a replying yell and then dove for Cara, his feet in the air as he wrapped his arms around her and sent them both flying off the end of the porch. He rolled, keeping her as close to him as he could.

He sat up, Cara limp in his arms, her eyes closed, face white as her head lolled against him, an arm dangling over his, her hair flowing around her. He called her name, getting no response. One of the off-duty paramedics ran towards him even as his partner ran towards the ambulance that sat there, two other on-duty paramedics splitting off from the group running towards him.

"Cara?" Corin could feel despair rising in him. She wasn't responding. "Cara? Please, Cara, wake up! Talk to me!"

He looked up as the paramedic, Tom he thought, knelt beside him, reaching for Cara.

"On the ground, Corin. We need her on the ground." He reached for her wrist, his face tightened as he spoke quietly to his friend, who nodded and reached for one of the boxes.

Corin was moved back, kneeling on the ground, before he sat back on his feet, his face white, fists clenched, tears he didn't know he was shedding creeping down his face. He heard the whispers around him, whispers that there had been an electrical charge to the knob, just waiting for one of them. Whoever had done it knew that Cara would be there that day.

A hand was laid on his shoulder and he heard murmurs around him, but his focus was solely on Cara. He gripped his hands tighter into fists as he saw the men working, trying to revive her, pulling out the defibrillator to shock her heart. He heard their murmurs and saw the heart monitor pulled out, the tube going down her throat, the IV lines being run. No, dear Lord, he prayed. Please, Lord, don't let her die. I'm not ready for this. He heard the angry and concerned mutters from the men and women who had gathered around them.

He heard the count as they finally gently lifted Cara to the stretcher and ran for the ambulance, Corin stumbling to his feet and following, not hearing the shouts that someone would take him there. He ignored the men, scrambling into the rig with her, his eyes on her face even as the paramedics continued to work on her, not giving up even though it seemed hopeless.

Two hours later, Corin sat, frozen in place, hands clenched together, eyes on the door behind which Cara lay, not moving from his spot. He heard Emma, Bruce, and Nigel moving around him and felt Emma's arm come around him.

"I'm sorry, Emma. I didn't know that would happen."

Bruce stood in front of him, before he crouched down, forcing Corin to look at him. Bruce shook his head, worry evident on his face. "You couldn't have known, Corin. Whoever this is has made it impossible for us to determine just what they're up to. You know that. All we can do right now is pray and trust."

Corin sat back, shoving his hands through his already tousled hair, catching Nigel's eye. Nigel shook his head, agreeing silently with his father. "I should have been the one. I should have been the one to go in."

"But they said you had all been in and out of there all morning. So, why was it that this happened at this time?" Nigel was puzzled.

"I have no idea." Corin shoved to his feet, unsteady for a moment, looking down at the crack in his cast. He hadn't realized he had fallen that hard and broken it.

Emma's hand touched his cast. "You need that looked at, Corin."

He shook his head. "Not until we know how Cara is." He blinked hard, not wanting the tears to fall again and start Emma's.

Instead, the tears fell, and Emma wrapped him into a hug, just as she would have her own son. Bruce looked around as he heard quiet footsteps and moved towards John, Nigel at his side. He didn't see Corin loose himself from Emma and follow.

"John?"

John shook his head. "It was meant to kill her, Bruce. I've taken a look and had the power company and an electrician out. Whoever it was wired up the door knob and put it on a timer. They didn't have to be on site for it to trigger. They worked the wire down the wall and across from the bottom hinge. It was blended in with the wood. No one would have seen in with a casual glance." He looked at the three men and then at Emma who stood, arm around her husband and son. "We think whoever it was had a camera set somewhere they could see when she went in on her own."

Corin spun in despair, his head going back as he looked up. Why, God? Why? Who would want to hurt our Cara? He spun back as he heard more footsteps.

The treating physician, Joe Lockyer, from church stood there, his eyes compassionate. Emma's hands flew to her mouth as she expected the worst. Joe turned, beckoning them to follow him. He shoved open the door to a board room and waited for them to enter.

"Joe?" Bruce's voice was steady but they could hear the fear in it.

"Bruce. She's alive. If she hadn't had treatment that quickly, I can't say that she would be. We're still assessing her to see what damage has been done. That's what's taking the time to get you back to see her. Soon, I promise." He looked around, searching for someone. "Who freed her from that door knob?"

Corin cleared his throat, then spoke. "I did. I didn't think. All I thought of was getting her away from it. I knew it. I hurt her more." Tears prickled behind his eyes once more at the thought.

Joe shook his head as he approached and set a hand on Corin's shoulder. "No, actually you didn't. She just had her fingertips on the knob for some reason, I doubt she'll even remember why. That helped, but your quick actions kept her from getting hurt worse. You weren't on the ground when you hit her, were you?"

Corin shook his head. "I really don't know. I ran for her and I think leapt for her, taking us off the end of the porch." He sank back against the table, his legs not able to hold him upright any longer, his eyes on Joe, hope springing into them. "I didn't hurt her any worse?"

"No, you didn't. Having the paramedics on site was what kept her alive, coupled with your actions." He went on to explain what they found and what heart testing they were needing to do. "I can't guarantee she won't have any lasting damage, though."

Bruce and Emma shared a long look, before Emma spoke. "We know that, Joe. Just let us see her. Please!" The worried mother turned to look at him, begging him silently to take them to her.

Joe sighed, jingling the change in a pocket, before he nodded. "Just two at a time and only for five minutes. Give me a couple of minutes and I'll be back for you two." He shut the door behind him, leaning against it for a moment, before he realized John stood there, keen eyes watching him.

"Joe?"

Joe shook his head. "I don't even know how she's still alive. The electrician stopped by. She should be dead, John. I can't even guarantee that she'll still make it even now and if she does that she won't have permanent damage of some kind."

John nodded.  "That's about what I thought you'd say.  Now what?"

"I get her parents back to her and then Nigel.  The other young man?"

"Corin?"

"Corin.  What's his relationship to her?"  Joe hadn't gotten to know Corin very well.

"Corin and Cara?  I'd say they are a couple.  Bruce let it slip that Corin had asked her to pretend but then changed his mind and wanted it to be real.  Cara talked to her folks and I know she was praying that way.  I don't know what the outcome has been."

Joe shook his head.  "I would say they're a couple, just by the devastation in him.  Any word on who did this?"

John sighed. "No, and I wish there was. This will set them back again. The volunteers have been pulled for today until we go over every cabin that they're working on.  They are not a happy crew about this. That family is well liked."

"They are.  They have been there for anyone and everyone that has needed their help over the years, going back to Bruce and Emma's parents and even further back, I'd warrant." Joe looked up as a nurse approached. "Amy?"

"We've run the tests you've asked for Joe. We're waiting for the results. You wanted to know when you could take family back."

"Thank you, Amy. I'll take her parents back in a moment. We'll need to move her up to the ICU soon. I'd suggest we do that before we take anyone to see her. Get her settled and hooked up to what we need."

Amy nodded. "I'll look after that, Joe. I'll personally take her there myself. She's been a good friend over the years."

Joe stared after Amy as she walked away. "You would never have known that, given how Amy acted in there, professional to a degree I don't see that often." He sighed. "Let me know what I can do."

"For one thing, make sure only approved personnel are allowed into her room. I'm stationing an officer there around the clock. They'll have a list and no one and I can guarantee no one who is not on that list will get through."

Joe nodded. "I'll personally make that list and get it to you." He nodded towards the officer that stood waiting. "Send him back in five minutes. We'll move her, then come get the family."

# Chapter 8

*H*ands jammed into his pockets, Corin hesitated at the closed door, his mind blank, but he somehow knew he was praying. He wasn't ready to go in and see her. Nigel had warned him that she was hooked up to a lot of machines. He didn't think he could see her like that but he knew he just couldn't not go in.

He nodded at the officer standing at the door, who reached and gently pushed the door open. He didn't see the look of compassion sent his way. His focus was on the walk into the room and then to the bed.

He stopped half way there, his eyes on the machines, listening to the beep of the monitors, the hiss of the ventilator, and his eyes sank closed. He had prayed she wouldn't need that. Dear Lord, please. He couldn't put into words his pleas, but he knew God heard his silent cries. This was one of those times his father told him that the Holy Spirit prayed for him, a time when he was so distraught he couldn't find the words he needed.

His feet finally moved forward, his eyes dropping to Cara, and he groaned. She was so white, he thought. He once more traced the equipment keeping her alive, not liking it one bit. His anger grew inside him. He needed to find who was responsible for this. His eyes dropped to her hand as he reached for it and clasped it in his own hand, seeking to warm the chill of it. He searched for her other hand, seeing it on top of the blankets, fingers wrapped against the burns she had suffered from the door knob.

He stood, his eyes on her face, his hand on her cheek, for how long he didn't know. He heard activity around him, vaguely seeing a nurse moving in or out before someone touched his shoulder and then led him from the room.

He leant against the wall, finally sliding down to sit on the floor, his head down on his upraised knees, his arms wrapped around them. He couldn't think, couldn't move, couldn't do anything. He finally felt himself pulled to his feet and then shoved gently into a chair.

He heard Nigel talking to him, but didn't listen to the words. He finally rose, his feet leading him from the building and to his car. Nigel stood and watched him, not sure where he was heading but also not sure if he should follow. He turned to look back at the hospital, then ran for his car, heading in the same direction that Corin had taken.

Corin parked near the cabin, his eyes not seeing it at first. He climbed out, heading for the door, before he realized Nigel was standing there, blocking his way.

"Out of my way, Nigel."

"You can't go in the, Corin. None of us can. John hasn't released it yet."

Corin spun, kicking at a clump of dirt, watching it crumble to pieces, just like his life he thought.

"Who did this, Nigel? Who hates her that bad?"

"Why would you think it's someone who hates her?" Nigel was clearly puzzled at Corin's words.

"This is not just a crime. Someone has put a lot of thought into it. I think it's been planned for years, just waiting for an opportunity. It may not be related to the bodies at all, you know."

Nigel stared at him. "You don't think so?"

Corin shook his head. "I don't. It might be but it seems overkill, to go after her for something she never saw."

Nigel finally nodded, leaning back against his truck. "Then, who?"

Corin spoke a name, causing Nigel to jerk upright and stare at him in shock. "There is no way it would be that person!"

"No? Says who? You may know the people in town, or think you do. I'm a stranger here. I see things differently, and that's how I see it."

Corin turned as he heard another voice. John stood behind him. "Corin? Who did you say?"

Corin repeated himself, watching John carefully, ready to defend himself.

"That's one person we are looking at." He held up his hand at Nigel's protest. "I know, Nigel. I know. But we have to look at everyone connected to her, past and present."

"I can assume, then, that you've cleared me?" Corin spoke half in jest, but he knew John would have looked into his background.

"I have." John turned to stare at the cabin. "Why this cabin?"

Nigel looked around. "Someone could have hidden in the trees and watched. They're close enough to give good sight but far enough away that we wouldn't have noticed anything." He shivered. "Were they that close to us?"

John turned, contemplating what Nigel had said. "You're right, Nigel. We searched the woods and found a spot where it looked as if someone had waited for a while. But there was no evidence there. We ran the dogs, but it ended up a dead end."

He turned as his phone rang, walking away as he took the call. Corin stared at the woods and then walked that way, Nigel at his side.

"What are we actually looking for, Corin?"

Corin shrugged. "I have no idea. I know John's people would have done a good search, but I still want to look."

He stared at the ground, turning to look back at the cabin. "This is where I think John pointed to. But it doesn't give a good line of sight, does it?"

Nigel agreed with him. "If we go further to our right."

Corin nodded, following along the tree line, until he finally stopped. "Here. You can see where Cara was working and then watch her walk to the cabin." He carefully walked into the trees, his eyes searching the area.

"There. What's that?" Nigel pointed at a piece of paper caught in a bush.

Corin reached for it, carefully pulling it out with his handkerchief. "It's a warning, Nigel. A warning that they're not done with her." He looked around, fear running through his body.

John stood for a moment, watching the two younger men before he spoke, his hand reached for the paper Corin held. "What do you have there, Corin?"

"A threat, John. You can see for yourself. And look. The ground is really disturbed here."

John sighed, knowing somehow they had missed this. "I'll call in the team. You two get back to your trucks and stay there. We'll need your statements."

Bruce stood for a moment, his eyes on the two younger men before he approached John.  A few moments of conversation and then Bruce walked towards them.

"Nigel.  Corin."

Nigel looked up from where he was fingering his keys. "Dad?  Is Cara worse?"

Bruce shook his head.  "The same. John called me.  He say you gave him a name, Corin."

Corin nodded.  "No one seems to like it though."  He turned, walking away, heading for his truck.  He needed to be alone, but he also needed to be with Cara.  He was torn as to where he should go.

Bruce watched him walk away.  "He's hurting, Nigel, and there is nothing we can to do help him, except pray for him, and be there is he wants to talk."

"I know, Dad.  He feels so responsible for what happened."

Bruce nodded, his thoughts going to the name Corin had given and then nodding to himself.  He could see that very easily. Now, how did they prove it?

# Chapter 9

*C*ara moved, discomfort on her face, as she tried to fight the machines keeping her alive. She felt like she was suffocating and pulled at the tube in her throat, a hand coming up to stop her. She didn't like that and fought the hand before darkness claimed her again.

Corin rested his hand on hers, waiting for her to rouse again. The nurses said she might rouse in the next few days. They would wait to pull the ventilating tube until they knew for sure she could breath on her own.

He turned as he heard footsteps. Emma watched her daughter for a moment.

"Did she wake up, Corin?"

He shook his head. "No, not really. She did try and pull the tube though. That's something she hasn't tried before."

"No, and she shouldn't. We'll have to watch her." She handed him the cup of tea she had brought him. "Go and sit and drink that. You're not doing her any good wearing yourself out."

He sighed. "I know, but I just can't leave her."

"Corin. Listen to me. You are not responsible for what happened. You've told us you watched her as much as you could. None of us suspected they'd go to this length."

He nodded, not convinced he wasn't responsible. "Have they said anything more about what could be wrong?"

Emma blinked back tears, knowing the grave and black possibilities that faced them. "No, they haven't, not in the last few days. They know they've gotten through to us on that." She turned, a puzzled look on her face. "Who brought in that package?"

"What package?" Corin's attention shifted to where Emma pointed. "That's new. I have no idea." He moved to look at it, then with a grim look on his face, headed for the door and the officer there.

Thirty minutes later, John stood in the room, watching as a tech removed the package. "You didn't see it brought in?" The question was directed at the officer.

"No, sir. I've watched everyone coming in and out of here and no one had that in their hands. Not that I saw. There hasn't even been cleaning staff in here over the last few hours."

"Then, how did it get in here? It just didn't appear on its own." John nodded as the tech approached. "Call me when you open it. Send photos as well. I want to know what it is when you know."

"Yes, sir. This has a priority."

Corin had been watching and listening. He vaguely remembered hearing wheels coming through the door before they stopped. He frowned as he studied the officer. Something was off and he wanted to know what.

"John? Can I talk to you outside for a moment?" Corin spoke quietly to John, nodding towards the door.

"Sure. We'll be back, Emma. And you." He pointed to the officer. "At the door. Watch every single person that tries to enter here. You know who is and isn't allowed." The officer nodded in a sulky manner and returned to his position outside the door.

John walked beside Corin towards the waiting room, pushing open the door to an empty room and then turning to face Corin.

"Corin? You've noticed something. After you finding that spot two days ago, I should hire you to the force."

Corin gave a quick grin even as he shook his head. "Not interested." Then he sobered. "About an hour ago, I remember hearing wheels at the opening door and then soft footsteps in the room. I was too engrossed in watching Cara fighting to come awake that I didn't look around. If I heard something, where was your officer?"

John tensed, knowing what Corin was asking and knowing he would have to follow up. He drew a deep breath. "Thank you, Corin, for keeping this quiet. I'll follow up. I'll have an officer pull the security tapes and see what we find out. I'm not confident, thought, that we'll find much." He paused, not sure how to continue. "How is Cara today?"

"She tried to wake up, tried to pull the breathing tube. We're afraid, John, afraid she won't come back to us."

John nodded. "That's a possibility, Corin, that I know everyone is praying against.  Trust God, son.  He's getting you through this."

"I know, but sometimes it's so hard to pray.  Dad has asked if I can come home next week for a few days.  I've told him no.  I need to stay here."

"Will they come to you instead?"

"I have no idea.  Mom is talking to Dad about that, so we'll see."  Corin paused, his hand on the door.  "Now what, John?  How much longer?"

"That's the question everyone wants the answer to and I don't have it."  John's hand rested for a moment on Corin's shoulder before Corin pulled the door open and walked away, not towards Cara, but towards the chapel.  He needed that time alone with God.

Corin slid into a back pew, his arms resting on the seat back in front of him, his eyes focused on the cross at the front.  He didn't think, couldn't put anything into words, but felt the presence of God there.  He buried his face into his arms and just rested, knowing that God would speak to him at some point.  He heard the door swish open quietly and then felt the pew ahead of him shift as someone sat, silent.

He finally raised his head and frowned. He didn't know the man who sat there, but the man seemed to know him.

"Corin? How are you, my friend?"

"Do I know you?"

The man nodded. "We met years ago. I'm a friend of your father's. Saul Adams."

Corin shook his head. "I'm sorry. I really don't remember you."

Saul laughed. "That's okay. I remember you. You're hurting, son, and that's why I'm here."

Corin studied the man, taking in the white hair and beard, the blue eyes, and frowned. "How did you know?"

"God told me. I knew I'd find you here." He paused, his eyes on his fingers as he rubbed them together. "What can I do for you? How can I help you?"

Corin gave a bark of laughter. "If I knew, I'd tell you. Can you bring Cara back to us, back to the way she was? Can you heal the hurts this has caused? Can you bring to justice the one who did this?"

Saul shook his head. "That's a lot to ask, Corin. What if she is never like she was?

Will you still love her or will you walk away?"

Corin sat in silence, his eyes returning to the front of the chapel. He frowned, noticing a glow around the cross he had not seen before. He knew there were no lights behind it. "I can, Saul. That I can. I can still love her. She's the other half of my heart." He looked back at the pew in front of him. Saul was gone.

Corin spun, staring around, his eyes searching for Saul. The door hadn't moved. He hadn't heard or seen Saul move and for Saul to leave, he would have had to pass through his line of sight. Corin's head dropped back to his arms. I get it, Lord. I really do.

Emma turned, startled as she felt a presence beside her and stifled a scream. She didn't know the man who stood there.

He gave a gentle smile at her. "I didn't mean to frighten you. My name is Saul. I heard about your daughter. May I pray with you?"

Unable to speak, Emma nodded, her eyes closing as she heard the soothing, quiet voice of the man. He finished but her eyes remained closed. They shot open as she realized she was alone. Spinning she stared the door and realized she had not heard it open or close.

Corin walked in a few minutes later, finding Emma with her hand on Cara's cheek, tears on her face. He stopped, his heart sinking. Emma turned, a smile on her face.

"She opened her eyes, Corin. Just now. She looked up at me and knew me. The nurse has gone to get the doctor."

Corin's feet propelled him to the end of the bed where he stood, his eyes on his treasure, waiting. "What happened, Emma? I know something did."

She paused, not quite sure of what she had seen. "A man was here and prayed for her. Then he was gone."

Corin's eyes shot to hers. "White hair? White beard? Blue eyes? Called himself Saul?"

She nodded, a question on her face.

Corin sighed. "He spoke with me in the chapel and then just disappeared. Is that what happened, Emma?"

She nodded. "It was. You don't suppose……". Her voice died away before she could finish her question.

Corin came around and hugged her. "God works in mysterious ways, Emma. I know that. So, yes, He may well have sent an angel. Or it could have just been a friend of my father's as he said."

"Your father has strange friends, then, that's all I can say." She looked up as the nurse came back.

"Dr. Lockyer is on his way in. He felt compelled to return, he said. About ten minutes." The nurse moved to take Cara's vitals, stopping as she realized Cara was watching her.

"Cara. You're awake. Dr. Lockyer will be here shortly and we'll see what we can do about some of this equipment. Would you like that?"

Cara nodded wearily before her eyes found her mother and then Corin, stopping as she saw him. He could tell she was trying to talk to him and rested his hand on hers, his fingers closing tight around her hand.

Joe Lockyer stepped back, swinging his stethoscope around his neck. "In all my years, I have never seen this. Never heard a tale like you've told me." He studied Cara. "We can pull the ventilator, I think, nurse and see how she makes out." He peered at the other monitors.  "It's like she was never hurt at all."

"God."  Corin's softly breathed sentence stopped Joe.

"It had to be, Corin.  That's the only explanation.  I would like to talk with that Saul."

Corin smiled at Emma, even as they both shook their heads.  "I doubt you'll find him, Joe.  He was here and gone."  Corin's eyes went back to Cara, finding the tube gone from her throat.

Emma moved closer, tears on her face, as she leaned over to gently hug her daughter.  "Thank you, Lord."

Three days later, Cara sat up in her bed, leaning back, oxygen prongs in place, IV still in her arm, as she watched Corin pace.  He's making me dizzy, she thought, and he's hovering.  How do I get him to leave for a while?

"Cara?"  Corin stood in the middle of the room, his eyes on her.

"Corin, you need to go do something. Find a hammer and pound some nails.  Pick up a saw or something.  You can't stay here forever."

He sighed, knowing she was right, but not wanting to leave her.  "I know, but I…"

She cut him off.  "It doesn't seem to matter if you're with me or not.  They find a way to reach me.  Now, go.  Don't come back for a whole day.  If you do, you won't get through that door."  She held up a finger as he protested.  "I mean it.  Twenty four hours.  Get some sleep.  Work on the cabins.  Do anything but hover over me."

He paused in his protest.  "That's what I'm doing, isn't it?"  At her nod, he walked towards her, his hand reaching out, waiting until she gave him hers.  "I'm sorry.  I just want to make sure you're all right."

"I know you do.  John has someone else on the door now.  The nurses know not to let anyone in.  Mom will be here soon and so will Dad.  Now go.  No, I mean it."

He finally nodded, bending over to drop a kiss on her forehead.  "I will, but under protest.  Twenty four hours and I'll be back."

"I know you will.  Now go."  She watched as he reluctantly walked to the door, turning to stare at her before the door closed behind him.  She laid her head back, fatigue weighing heavily on her. A movement in the room brought her head up, fear coursing through her.

"Who are you?" She stared at the man standing there.

"My name is Saul. Sorry. I didn't mean to frighten you."

"Well, you did. How did you get in, anyway? I know you're not on the list."

Saul smiled, a gentle smile that warmed her. "How, that's not important. I just wanted to let you know that God has heard the pleas of your family and friends. He has healed you in a way that you shouldn't be healed."

She looked down for a second and when she looked back up, he was gone. She stared around, shocked, fear coursing through her until she felt a gentle touch on her arm, a touch from someone not there. Her eyes raised to the ceiling

"God, I know you have angels around. Was Saul one of them? I know I shouldn't even be here, that I should be dead. Now, what is it You've left me here to do?"

*Chapter 10*

Corin watched carefully as Cara moved around the living room at home, not sure if she should have come home so soon, but she had insisted and the physicians really didn't have a reason for her to be in hospital. She turned as her mother spoke to her and then headed for the kitchen. Corin followed, knowing that John was there and wanted to talk to them.

Cara stared at John for a moment before she sighed. "No news, is there, John?"

He smiled. "Actually, we do have some. I'm just waiting for your Dad to come back."

Nigel stood, back to the counter, his eyes on his sister. Corin slid into a chair beside her and took the hand she reached out. Her fingers were cold and he didn't like that.

Bruce stood at the back door, assessing the group for a moment before he spoke. "John? You said you had news?"

John nodded. "I do. The parcel that was left? It contained pictures of Cara about town and your property. She is being followed. There is nothing so far that we've found to lead us to whoever this is."

Nigel spoke. "I don't think it's Tam. I talked to a friend of his. Tam moved overseas years ago and hasn't been back since. His parents don't even hear from him."

John nodded. "We've heard that. We're working with those authorities to confirm his whereabouts. His parents refuse to talk to us. We're watching them, though."

Corin shared a look with Cara, who nodded, knowing what he was about to ask. "What if it's not, Tam? Or his family? What if it's someone else?"

John nodded again, his eyes on Corin. "We've considered that. It's more than likely the correct supposition, but we need to do a lot more investigative work to get to someone." He turned to Cara, concerned at her white look and the dark rings of fatigue under her eyes. "Cara? This is where we need your help. We need to know everyone who might have a grudge against you, who might want to hurt you. Even if you discount the person because of friendship, list that name and who they are to you."

She nodded before her head rested against Corin's shoulder and she yawned. "I can do that, just not right now. I don't think I can see a piece of paper to write on."

Her family smiled even as John shook his head at her. Corin gave a low sound and then swept her into his arms, heading for her bedroom, Emma on his heels.

"Here, Corin. Let me pull the blankets back. She'll be up again soon, if I know her." Emma tucked her daughter in, then stepped back to wrap an arm around Corin. "She's here with us, Corin. She shouldn't be. You can't continue to blame yourself."

He gave an abrupt nod. "I know I shouldn't but I still think there is something I could have done."

Emma shook her head. "If you had been with her, perhaps neither one of you would have survived." She turned him, drawing him out of the room and back to the kitchen. "Let's hear what John has planned for us. I'm sure he has something."

Cara rose later that day, her eyes feeling heavy from fatigue and worry. She stood, her eyes searching her room, feeling something off but now sure what. She walked towards her bookshelves, her fingers running over the books until she found her yearbook from her last year of high school.

She sat back on the bed, drawing a deep breath, not quite ready to open a book she hadn't opened in years but knowing she had to. Her fingers traced faces as she turned the pages, finally stopping at her own graduating class, her finger moving from face to face until she stopped, dread coursing through her. She knew who it was now, who it was that was haunting her. To tell John would not be easy. That she knew already. She didn't have proof, just a feeling and he couldn't investigate anything based on just feelings.

Nigel had stopped at her half-open door, watching, before he used his fingertips to shove the door open all the way. He sat beside her, not saying a word, waiting for her to speak. When she didn't, he leaned over to look at the photos, drawing in a deep breath as he saw the one she still had her finger on.

"That one, Cara? You're sure?"

She nodded, her face full of sorrow. "I think so, Nigel. It makes sense, doesn't it?" She looked up, fear lurking in her eyes. "How do I tell anyone?"

"Not yet. Let me look into it. Corin will want to help as well." He held up a hand at her protest. "He will and you won't be able to stop him once he hears this." He shot a look behind him as he heard a sound and saw Corin standing in the hallway, a question in his face. "Talk to him, Cara. Tell him what it's all about. It's only fair. If they can't get to you, they'll go after him. They've been watching you two."

She nodded, a sigh escaping. "I guess I can't really avoid that, can I?" She stood, turning to walk away when she saw Corin. "Corin? How long have you been there?"

"Just now." He stretched out his hand, a grin appearing on his face. "Come on. We need to do something fun. Enough doom and gloom."

"Doom and gloom?" She smiled slightly. "Is that what this is?"

"It is," He tucked her arm into his and led her to the kitchen. "I'm cooking tonight." He held up his hand at the look she shot him. "I can cook, I'll have you know. Not a lot but there is one recipe that is mine. No one else has it."

"A secret recipe, is it?" She slid onto one of the stools at the counter. "And just why would you need my help?" She grinned as she watched him choose her mother's fussiest apron, with all the frills and ruffles, and tie it on. "Really, Corin? That one?"

"Of course this one," he responded, nose in the air in a snooty manner as he ran his hands along the ruffles. "The apron is all part of the secret recipe, you know."

"Okay. So, what do I have to do?"

"Not a thing, except sit there and look pretty." He laughed at the face she made, thinking that she really didn't know how beautiful she was. He walked around the counter, coming to stand beside her, an arm around her. When she looked up, he dropped a kiss on her cheek, walking away to find his ingredients, not realizing that she sat, hand to her cheek, her mouth slightly open, her eyes on him. He really didn't know he made her feel so wanted.

"Okay, so it looks as if I have everything." He dropped an assortment of vegetables and chicken on the counter, reaching for a skillet and began sorting through his food stuffs and then chopping and slicing and frying before he dumped it all into a baking dish and sliding it into the oven.

"And just what do you call that?"

He shrugged. "I've never come up with a name for it. When Mom and Dad ask for it, it's just called that thing you make with no name."

She laughed even as she shook her head, before turning as she heard voices. She froze for a moment, knowing John was there.

"Cara? How are you now?" John approached her, sitting next to her.

"I have no idea how I'm supposed to be. Do you?" She was genuinely puzzled by them asking her that all the time.

"No, I don't either. Listen. I need to talk to you about something." He looked up at Corin, who removed the apron and went to leave.

Corin caught the look on Cara's face and just couldn't walk away. Standing behind her, hands on her shoulders, he waited.

"We've been searching for a culprit, as you know. There is one name that keeps coming up again and again." He didn't want to tell her but had no choice.

"Lizzie." She looked up at him, seeing his surprise. "I came to that conclusion this afternoon. Nigel knows. He asked me to talk to you."

"Lizzie and Beth. They were close, weren't they?"

"They were sisters, but I didn't think they were that close. They were so different." She shuddered. "Have you talked to Lizzie?"

John shook his head. "We can't find her. We know she's been in and out of her house. We've seen the evidence of that. I'm trying to get enough to obtain a warrant for her house, but it's difficult." He paused, his eyes on the window across from him. "Have you heard from Beth?"

"Not since she and Tam left. I haven't heard if she's come back to town. Her parents blamed me for some reason, even though I had nothing to do with that."

"They do. They've been vocal about that with me over the years."

Corin finally spoke. "What makes you think it's this Lizzie?"

"That's all part of the investigation that I can't talk about, but I can tell you that we have been given letters and photos written and taken by her that implicate her in what's been happening. What we can't do is link her to the skeletons you found."

John finally stood, heading out, leaving the young couple to face one another.

"Why Lizzie?" Corin was puzzled.

"Because she has a very vindictive streak and wouldn't think anything about going after someone who hurt her family. I just don't see why she would wait this long. That doesn't make sense."

Corin moved the stove, taking the baking dish from it, sending aromas through the kitchen that soon had the rest of the family heading that way. He was puzzled, and troubled, by what Cara had said. It just didn't make any since. He would have to look into this, he thought.

Cara watched as Corin worked away, knowing she would have to talk with him soon. Her feelings for him were rising, he made her feel that beautiful and special, but she wasn't sure exactly how he felt or if it was just guilt.

Corin looked up, catching her eyes on him, and then nodding. "We'll talk, Cara love, and soon. Right now, there's a piece of paper and pen. Do what John asked earlier. Put down any and all names you can think of, even if you don't suspect they'd do what's been happening."

"That's the thing, Corin. I can't see anyone I know doing this. I just don't get the why of it."

"I know you don't. Neither do I." He paused, a thought coming to his mind. "What about people who have stayed here? Anyone from them come to mind?"

She shook her head, then paused. "No. Yes. Maybe." She looked as him as he started to laugh. "I know. Real positive, wasn't I? There was a couple about ten years ago? None of us felt comfortable around them for some reason." She reached for the pen and paper and began to do just what John had asked of her.

*Chapter 11*

$\mathcal{T}$wo weeks later, Cara moved carefully through the cabins, Corin beside her, as she inspected them, her family one cabin ahead of her.

"They're all done and ready to open next week, Corin. I didn't think we'd make it."

His arm around her, he nodded. "That we did. We had so many volunteers, especially after you were hurt. We almost had too many at times." He paused, his eyes following the flight of a bird they had disturbed when they walked out of that cabin before he sighed. "I talked to John this morning. He's still not that far ahead. It's frustrating."

"I know it is, but we just have to keep moving forward. One of these days, they, whoever it is, will show themselves and we'll find them. Now, what will you be up to?"

"I've some work lined up in town. But what about you? You're not strong enough yet to continue working at the camp."

"No, I'm not. I'm not really sure that I want to anyway. This has given me a chance to think and evaluate my life. I just kind of fell into working here. Mom and I have talked. Come the fall, I'm looking at taking more college courses, in what yet, I'm not sure."

"Interior design. Decorating." He paused their walk, his eyes on hers. "Please, just don't walk away from me."

She stared up at him. "Corin? Just what are you saying? You've been dropping hints now for weeks."

He bit his lip, knowing that if he said how he felt, she might walk out of his life and that wouldn't do at all. "You're a beautiful lady, Cara love. More beautiful than I think you realize. You've come to mean the world to me. Yes, I'll admit it. I'm in love with you. There! You've made me say it!" He abruptly moved away from her, to stand near the pond and stare moodily in it.

Cara watched him for a moment, her hands to her mouth, not quite sure she had heard right. He loved her? Oh, glory! Then it wasn't a one-way street of love.

"Corin." Cara stood behind him, not quite touching him, but close enough that she could if she wanted to. "I'm not mad. In fact, I'm glad you said what you did. You see, I've been in love with you for years. I just didn't know it. Forgive me for the way I acted. I was afraid you wouldn't feel the same."

Corin had turned as she spoke, his eyes on her, before he reached and hugged her to him. "We'll take it slow, love, just as slow as we need. We have our whole life."

"We do, but only God knows how long that is." Cara leaned against him. "We have to go find the others you know."

"I know." He looked down at her, desperately wanting to kiss her but knowing it wasn't the right time. Not yet.

Emma watched as the two made their way towards them, hand in hand, and turned to Bruce, who nodded. They shared a smile before Nigel's voice called to them from the kitchen.

"Dad. Mom. Someone's been in here while we were out." His voice was grim. "John's on his way."

Bruce stood, staring at the box on the kitchen table. Nigel was right. That had not been there before. "Any name on it?"

"Cara's. And Corin's." Nigel turned to watch the two, seeing Cara's face paling at his words. "Whoever it is just walked right in here."

Cara turned into Corin, letting him wrap her in his arms. "When will it ever end?"

John stood later, watching a tech open the box, shooting glances at the five standing near the counter. He sighed to himself. This was getting old, he thought. We need this over with.

"John?" The tech motioned him over.

He peered into the box, not prepared to see what he saw. A baby doll? Covered in red paint, at least he hoped it was paint. The tech finished taking the photos he needed, and then carefully felt around the doll, pulling out a plastic bag with an envelope in it.

"Photograph it and take it out for me, please." John was not happy. The investigation had just shifted and he wasn't sure who he was after any more.

He read the letter, anger starting to burn within him. He snapped a quick photo before nodding to the tech, who bagged everything and was gone.

"John?" Cara's voice reached him. "What was in that?"

He turned, his keen eyes searching each one's face, seeing the fear, the anxiety, the stress. "A baby doll, Cara, covered in red paint. And a letter."

Cara's face paled even more. "Beth?" She sought Nigel's eyes for a moment. "Did Beth's baby survive, Nigel? I don't remember."

Nigel shook his head. "I have no idea, Cara. I never heard." He looked at John. "Do you know?"

John shook his head. "The baby died when he was only three months old. The report said SIDS but that there were unexplained bruises and marks. We're having the medical examiner there look back into it." He looked back at Cara. "That could be a motive." He glanced at his phone, not ready to share the disturbing letter that threatened more and more violent acts against Cara and against Corin.

"The letter, John?" Emma's voice was strained.

"Threats against Cara and Corin." He looked at each one of them. "We need all of you to take precautions. Don't be out and about by yourself if you can help it. Keep a phone or radio on you at all times. Cara. Corin. This is especially true for you. If they can't get to Cara, they'll go after Corin."

John finally walked away, leaving the family in terror and anger. Cara swiped at the tears on her face before running to her bedroom. She stood, once more feeling something off in there. Corin watched from her doorway as she turned in a circle, finally stopping when she saw him.

"What's wrong in here, Cara? Something is. You've mentioned it before."

She shivered, wrapping her arms around herself. "There is, and I just can't pinpoint it." She turned, her eyes going to the pictures on the wall. "Corin, can you lift the pictures down? I need to take a good look at them."

They worked their way through her room, searching everything, before Corin reached for a doll on her shelf. "How long have you had this one?"

Cara froze, now knowing what was wrong. It wasn't her doll. She had never seen it before.

"It's not mine, Corin. I never had one like that."

Corin spun, the doll in his hand, before he reached for her arm and dragged her from the room, the doll in his hand.

"Stay here," he ordered as he ran from the kitchen and flung the doll away from him, hitting the ground as it exploded. He raised his head and then rose, running back for the house, Cara into his arms as he hit the kitchen. She sobbed as her family ran to find out what was going on.

"A bomb, Bruce. There was a bomb in a doll on her shelf. It's been there for weeks. I saw it whenever I walked by. I didn't know." Corin was berating himself for not knowing.

"None of us did, Corin." Bruce wrapped an arm around his wife and placed a hand on Nigel's shoulder. "We'll need John back." He sighed. "I'm guessing the doll exploded totally."

Corin gave a harsh laugh before shaking his head. "I threw it. I have no idea. And I can only hope I didn't damage anything when I threw it. I could only think about getting it out of the house."

Bruce nodded, his keen eyes on Corin. What was it about this young man, he thought, that made him trust him so thoroughly? It wasn't just that he had been in his home so often and was a good friend to Nigel. No, there was something more and he couldn't figure it out.

"Now what, Dad? How do I stay safe?" Cara paced, her arms wrapped around her. "And don't say you'll send me away. I won't go. Besides I can't, not with the doctors' appointments that I have to go to." She turned, catching Corin watching her.

Corin looked over at Bruce, nodding his head. It was time to have a family meeting, he decided, and come up with a plan. He didn't like the idea of Cara being afraid, but he realized that without knowing who it was, they were limited in planning.

# *Chapter 12*

*C*ara walked around the camp a few weeks later.  It was mid-summer and usually a time she enjoyed.  Not this year, she thought.  She was still recovering from her electrocution and that had taken a lot from her.  She was also living in fear, trying not to show it to her family, but she knew they were aware of how she felt.  How she didn't know was how she quite felt about Corin.  He was becoming a big part of her life, drawing her into his work with referrals from the homeowners he was working with.  She appreciated the work, but was still hesitant to work with him, not sure if what he had said was true.  He hadn't referred to his love for her again.

She turned as she heard her name called, seeing Peter running towards her.  He slid to a stop, a smile on his face.

"Cara!  You're a hard person to find."

"I am?  I didn't know that."  She hugged hm, then stood watching him.  "Now that you've found me, what do you want?"

"I just wanted to spend some time with you.  What were you up to?"  He grinned as she shook her head.

"I was just walking through, checking to make sure everything was the way it should be and seeing where we needed to do maintenance."  She stopped, her eyes on the pond and sighed.  "It looks as if we'll have to do maintenance there at some point."

Peter followed her line of sight and frowned.  "Don't you have your boats out?"

She turned to him, then looked again at the pond.  "We should do.  The canoes and kayaks for sure.  Why?"

"Because I don't see them, and I know you have a class coming up shortly."  He walked quickly to the pond, his eyes searching before he groaned.  "You won't be having a class today, Cara.  The canoes and kayaks are ruined."

"Ruined?  What do you mean?"  She followed his pointing finger and groaned.  "Now what?  And who would do that?"

"It's been quiet around here for a few weeks.  They're back, whoever they are. Now, let me call Dad and let him know."

Bruce stood, his arm around his daughter, staring as the canoes and kayaks were dragged ashore, seeing the damage that had been done to them, deliberate damage, he knew

"John?"

"This had to have happened overnight, didn't it, Bruce?  Cara said you used them yesterday.  Did you put in the security cameras like we had talked about?"

"I did, but it won't do you any good. Someone sabotaged the ones here."

John sighed, knowing he had little to go on.  "Did any of the others pick up movement?"

"Not that will help."  Bruce looked around.  "I suspect they came in from over there and then went back that way."  He pointed at the woods.  "And with the dry weather, we won't find much of a trail."

Cara stood for a moment, her eyes narrowed, before she moved off, her father and John following, Peter watching from where he stood near the shore.

"Dad, what's that?" Cara pointed towards a tree. "That wasn't there before."

"No, it wasn't. Stay here, Cara. Let John go look at that."

John walked towards the object Cara had seen, his heart sinking as he realized what it was. Another body. He approached, eyes searching the area, before he stooped to look at who it was. Lizzie! No wonder he hadn't been able to find her lately. He had talked to her finally about a week ago.

He sighed, knowing this just threw a wrench into his day and the investigation. Now who would they suspect?

He walks back towards Cara and Bruce, motioning them to turn around and walk back towards the cabin. He beckoned to Peter who came at a run. A few quiet words and Peter was standing guard over the body

"John?" Bruce's voice was quiet.

"It's Lizzie, John. She's dead."

Cara drew in a deep breath. "Dead? How?"

"We'll get the medical examiner out but it's likely been in the last twelve hours, about the time your canoes were sabotaged."

John turned to draw a line with his eyes from the body to the pond. "She may not be the one responsible, or she may have been. We can't tell yet."

Cara shuddered, hearing that someone she knew was dead. "Is it because of me?"

John shook his head. "I have no idea, Cara. We'll have to investigate and see what we can determine. We'll need to take statements from all of you about where you were from yesterday to now." He held up a hand as Cara opened her mouth. "Not a word, Cara. Not until we get your statements." He walked away, pulling out his phone as he did so.

Corin pulled up to the house that evening, noting the activity going on around it. He frowned, not having heard what had happened that afternoon. Nigel approached him, a grim look on his face.

"Nigel? What is going on? Is Cara all right?"

"She's fine, Corin. They found Lizzie's body in the woods near the pond after finding all the canoes and kayaks destroyed. We've had to do damage control like you wouldn't believe."

"I can see that." Corin raised his eyes, to see Cara approaching. "How is she?"

"She's hurting, Corin. Can you get her away for a few hours, she needs that."

"I can do that." He smiled and reached to draw Cara into a hug.

Cara clung to Corin, feeling safe where he was. He drew back, his eyes following her face, seeing the stress there.

"Come on, Cara love. Into the truck. We're going out for dinner. I hope you haven't eaten yet."

"No, actually I don't have much of an appetite."

"Then, come and keep me company." He tucked her into his truck and then slid behind the wheel.

"Why are you doing this, Corin? Did Nigel ask you to?"

He looked at her, not surprised at her question and shrugged. "He asked, but I had already decided on my way here to ask you to go for a drive tonight, just so we could spend some time together. It's been a while since we done that."

She stared at him for a moment before she nodded. "Okay, if that's what you say, I believe you. Where were you planning on eating?"

"In town at the Hollytown cafe." He began to laugh. "Somehow, eating at that cafe in the middle of July just doesn't make sense."

"I know. It really doesn't. But what can you say when that's the name of the town?"

She watched as he ordered, content just to be with him, although she could have done with him sitting on the other side of the booth, but he just had to sit beside her, grinning as she commented on that. Now the people in town would really be talking about them.

"Relax, Cara. It's okay. I think of you as my lady. I have for months now." He reached for her left hand, tracing her ring finger. "I think I need to put something here."

She stared at him, wonder in her eyes. "Just what are you asking, Corin?"

He looked around and gave a frustrated sigh. "This is not where I wanted to ask or how." He looked back at her, his love shining in his eyes. "I love you, Cara. I have for years. Will you consider my suit, let me court you, as they used to say?"

She looked at him for a moment, surprise then joy flooding through her. She never expected this. Not with all the trouble she thought she had caused him.

She finally nodded and he grinned, swooping in for a quick kiss. She stared at him, her hand going to her mouth.

"We'll take this up later, love. Right now, let me eat. Are you sure you don't want anything?"

She finally nodded. "Sure, but just a sandwich. Today kind of took away my appetite."

"About today. You'll need to explain. Nigel told me some. You weren't there, were you?" He groaned as she nodded. "Cara. How do we keep you safe when you keep getting into trouble?"

She shrugged. "I have no idea, Corin. I just wish this was all over."

Nigel watched from the porch as Corin helped Cara from the truck, her hand tucked in his as they walked towards the house.

"Cara. Corin." His voice caught their attention, and they abruptly stopped their conversation and their walk, sharing a glance before moving towards him.

"Nigel? It's late. Don't you have to be up and on the road early in the morning?" Cara's voice was quiet, given the late hour.

"I do, but I wanted to warn you. John will be back in the morning. He's got a laundry list of questions for you, Cara, about Lizzie and Beth. He's found evidence that Beth has been back in town for a while now and that she's been running with a rough crowd while she was away. Somehow he's tied it to what has been happening here over the last few months."

"Beth? I can't see that."

"I can. From what I understand, she would have a grudge against you, Cara." Corin's statement had her turning to face him.

"You can?"

"Sure. She ran off with Tam and then he left her. I can pretty much guarantee what a lot of fights they had would be and that would have been over you."

Cara stared at him, dumbfounded at his words. "You think? I was surprised when Tam left with Beth. He didn't seem to like her much, resented the times we would spend together."

Nigel nodded, understanding where Corin was headed with his statements. "What Corin is saying, Cara, is that Tam likely threw it up at Beth that she wasn't you, that he wanted you and you refused him in some way. So he settled for second best in his eyes and Beth refused to be second best."

Cara's eyes grew troubled and she leaned against Corin. "You think that?" She drew a troubled breath. "Then that explains a lot."

"What do you mean, Cara?" Nigel pointed to the chairs. "Sit. We need to talk this out tonight and then you need to talk to John when he comes in the morning. Corin, you might as well plan on using your room here. It's already late."

Corin gave a quick grin, even as he drew Cara down beside in the love seat and close to his side. "That's what I was figuring on. I have a bag in the truck."

"Prepared, are you?" Cara accepted the quick kiss he gave her, not seeing the speculative glance Nigel threw them. "To go back to what we were talking about, Nigel, you're right." She drew a troubled breath. "Tam pressured me to do things I wouldn't do and didn't like it when I refused. He wanted me to try drugs and alcohol. That's what we had been arguing about. I told him I wouldn't and that if he was I would not go out with him any more and that he couldn't come around. He left in anger that night. Beth had been secretive and a few times it seemed she was high or drunk. I could smell alcohol on her a few times and she always laughed it off. She changed those last few months of high school. Did you notice that?"

Nigel nodded. "I thought she was changing but I put that down to being almost finished high school and then heading off to college. I guess it wasn't, was it?" He paused, not quite sure how to continue.

"If you thinking of the rumours going around at the time, I heard them and confronted her. She denied them, but the truth was in her eyes. She played us, Nigel. She pretended to be such a good Christian and wasn't."

Nigel reached for his sister's hand and began to pray, asking for God's leading and protection, and for wisdom in how to continue their investigation. Corin took up the petition when Nigel finished, Cara tight under his arm. He wanted to protect her but knew he couldn't be with her at all times.

They finally rose, heading for the house, quiet good nights sounding. Cara dropped to her bed, pulling a light blanket over her, not even bothering to change. She was asleep quickly, her left hand tucked up under her cheek, a smile on her face as she dreamed of Corin.

Corin stood for a while, contemplating their conversation with Nigel. How had this happened, Lord, his heart cried. How did people turn like that? The more he got to know Cara and the more he heard about her friends, the more concerned he grew. He knew it was only a matter of time before the events and danger escalated. Would they be prepared? They had already proven, whoever they were, that they really didn't care if people got hurt or died.

Cara stood, watching John the next morning, as he made notes from what she had said. John hadn't realized the pressure Cara had been under when she was that young or he would have stepped in. He'd want to talk to Peter about what she had said.

"Beth was into drugs? Was she part of the group that was breaking and entering?" John looked up at the sound Cara made, seeing the distress in her face.

"She likely was, John.  Some of the people she had started hanging around with, there were rumours about.  I never knew for sure.  I kept my distance. Besides I wanted to finish my studies with as high as marks as I could and I didn't have time or interest in the parties she wanted to attend."  Cara sighed.  "Do you think she's back working with some of them?"

John nodded.  "More than likely.  I have someone working on that supposition.  He'll know more by tomorrow, we hope."  He looked around, then motioned for her to sit.  "We haven't had a good talk in a while, Cara, other than about this stuff.  How are you really doing?"

She sighed, knowing he really cared about her.  "I'm struggling, John, trying to understand why God has let this happen.  It's hard, you know, to go through this and not know who it is that's behind it."

John agreed.  "It is.  But one good thing has come out of it."  He grinned at her frown.  "You and Corin have become a couple."

She sighed.  "You heard about our date last night."

He laughed.  "Actually I was in the diner.  You two didn't see me.  You were really engrossed in one another." He laughed again at her look. "Don't look at me like that. I was sitting in the diner already when you came in. I was not following you."

She laughed with him. "Yes, Corin has been a blessing. We've talked to Mom and Dad, but aren't saying any official yet. We are a courting couple, as they used to say."

"Wonderful, Cara. God has blessed you with a wonderful young man." John reached to hug her. "He'll take care of you. When he almost lost you, I thought he'd go crazy."

"That's what he said before. I didn't get it until last night." She sighed. "Can we end this, whatever it is, soon?"

He agreed, reaching for his phone as it rang, and excusing himself to answer it. A quick word and he was on his way out the door, Cara staring after him.

# Chapter 13

*H*esitating before he approached her, Corin watched Cara sitting on the ground of the church, a toddler on her knee, talking with one of the younger women at church. He couldn't place her name but he knew he'd find out before the day was through. He had become very protective of his lady since he had asked to court her a number of weeks ago. That was going just fine, he thought. He just needed to convince her he was serious and to move on to the next step.

Cara looked up, feeling eyes on her, frowning, her gaze searching until it stopped near a tree. Her heart sank. He was back. No matter what they said, he was back. That meant he would be coming for her. She felt someone drop to the ground beside her and turned, seeing Corin there, his hand reaching out the take the toy the little girl was handing him, a grin on his face, introducing himself to the girl's mother.

She sat, trying hard to keep her emotions locked inside her but knew she had failed where Corin was concerned. The mom and daughter finally rose at a call from her husband and walked away, leaving Corn and Cara still seated on the ground. Corin finally turned to her, seeking to find an answer on her face.

"Who was it, Cara? Who did you see?"

"How did you know I saw anyone?"

"I can tell, love. I'm getting to know you that well."

She sighed. "Tam. He's back in town and was standing there watching me. I'm sure he's the one who sabotaged the canoes in the summer." She turned to him. "I'm a dangerous person to be around, Corin."

Corin nodded. "And he's gone now, isn't he, love? He showed himself and then moved away."

She sighed, her head coming down on his shoulder. "I'm afraid, Corin. I'm afraid he'll hurt you. If what we've seen is what he's capable of, how do we stay safe?"

Corin shrugged, not quite sure of the answer. "That's something we'll discuss, love. But first. Let's you and I take a drive somewhere, just you and me. It feels like forever since we've had time alone."

She began to laugh, just as he hoped she would. "What do you mean? Didn't last night count?"

"Oh, that was last night. This is today." He rose, his hand helping her up and tucking hers tight inside his own, he walked her to his truck, frowning as he saw John standing there. "This isn't good, love. John's waiting for us."

She sighed, knowing that their afternoon had likely just disappeared.

"Corin. Cara. I was hoping to see you two alone." John was hesitant to speak, knowing he would totally destroy their day.

"We figured that when we saw you. What do you need to talk to us about?"

John shifted so he was leaning against the truck. "I've heard that Tam is back in town and looking for you, Cara."

"You're a little late with that warning, John. He's already found me." She looked up, her face pale. "He was here, watching me from across the parking lot. He didn't approach, but I suspect that it's only a matter of time before he does."

Corin looked past her, a frown on his face. "John, is that Tam over there?"

"Where?" John spun and headed the way Corin had indicated.

"Let's get you out of here. John will find us." Corin tucked her into the truck and then slid behind the wheel, not quite sure where to go. What had just happened had changed their plans.

"Where to now, Corin? I don't think you really want to drive anywhere."

He shook his head. "No, I don't. Not until John tells me he's talked to Tam." He sighed. "Guess it's back to your place, then."

"It's nice today, early fall. I can put us up a lunch and we can head for the pond."

Hours later, Corin sat up from where he had thrown himself on the ground beside Cara. "Now, what, Cara? Where do we go from here?"

She paused, not quite sure how to phrase what she wanted to say. "I'm not quite sure what you're asking, Corin. About us or about what's happening?"

"The what's happening to us we can't change or control. That's a given. I mean about us. Where do you see us going?"

"I just knew you'd ask that." She shook a finger at his grin. "I can see us growing old together, if we survive this. I feel like my life is on hold right now, Corin. Even though I know I'm moving ahead and doing things and studying it just doesn't see right."

Corin studied her face. "I know what you mean. We feel like we're stuck for now, waiting for the proverbial other shoe to drop. I say we forget about that, start planning a life together and face whatever it is at each other's side." He reached into his pocket, pulling out a ring and reaching for her hand. He bit his lip, trying to stem the flow of emotion and not quite succeeding. "Cara, I love you. Will you be mine for as long as we have? After almost losing you, I can't live without knowing if you will." He looked up at the silence.

Cara sat, tears sparkling in her eyes, matching the sparkle of the small diamond on the ring. She finally nodded. "I will, Corin."

Two hours later, they hunted up her parents, who were not surprised. Nigel just asked how come it took them so long.

A ringing of the doorbell sent Emma to the door, a surprised look on her face. "John? We weren't expecting you tonight. Come in. Corin and Cara just got engaged."

John grinned. "They did? We all suspected they would, just not so soon. Where is everyone?"

"In the kitchen, just about to sit down for supper. Come on in and join us." She stopped, the smile leaving her face for a moment. "You have word, don't you?"

He nodded, a grim look coming over his face for a moment. "I do. But it can wait until we eat. We'll need some time to go over everything." Her eyes found the folder he lifted slightly.

"I don't like the sounds of that, John, but come. Let's eat and then we plan."

John finally sat back, watching the young couple across from him, Cara's face flushed with happiness. He hated to destroy what should be a wonderful day for her, but he felt he had no choice. Time was of the essence and that he knew only too well. Reports had been coming in over the last couple of days and he had been working overtime to compile them.

"John?" Corin's voice held a question. "You're not just here to congratulate us, are you?"

He shook his head. "No, I'm not, and I wish I was. I talked to Tam, Cara. He says he's not behind what's happening. But I still need to verify his whereabouts over the summer and he's not saying where he was."

She nodded. "I don't think he will. Not unless there's something in it for him. And that something would be money. That's what always drove him. I still can't believe I saw anything in him."

"He hid was he was really like, Cara. None of saw that in him." Emma reached for her daughter's hand, rubbing it lightly. "I am just so thankful he's out of your life."

"I am too, Mom, but I still don't think he is. I think he's involved in this somehow, only I don't know how to find that out."

"Let John do that." She looked up as the doorbell rang, and hear Bruce answering it. She heard a familiar voice and saw Cara pale, rising and backing away.

Tam stood in the doorway, his eyes on Cara. She couldn't read the look on his face and she really did not want to talk to him.

"Leave, Tam. You have no business here."

"Oh, I think I do. I hear you've been spreading lies and rumours about me."

She snorted. "Not me. Now leave." Her eyes traced past him to Corin, who stood there, tall and strong, compared to the shorter and overweight Tam. "Corin, Tam was just leaving. Escort him out please. And then alert John that he was here."

Tam shrugged off Corin's hand. "I said I wasn't leaving, but your family can. You and I are going to have a talk, all by ourselves."

Corin reached for Tam's arm, and catching him, dragged him from the room and then through the house to the door. "Cara has said no. As far as I'm concerned, she's the boss and she has said she doesn't want to talk to you."

Tam turned, fists clenched and raised, spluttering. Corin looked past him, nodding to John.

"Tam. Just the person I've been looking for. I think it would be a good idea for you to come with me."

Tam shook his head. "Not happening. I'm heading back in to talk to Cara."

"She's refused, John, and asked him to leave. We had to remove him from the house."

John nodded. "Yes, I can see that." His hand reached for Tam's arm and Tam struggled, striking John in the face and causing him to lose his balance.

Tam shoved him away and headed once more for the house. Corin tackled him, taking him down, and bending one arm up behind his back. With a muttered word of thanks, John clamped handcuffs on Tam and hauled him to his feet, shoving him into the back of his cruiser.

"That will put him away for a bit, but he'll be out soon enough. I'll look into a restraining order against him."

"Thanks, John. Let me know if you need anything."

"We'll need your statement about this. That's one thing. Second, watch your lady in there. Things are heating up, is all I can tell you, and she's in more danger now that she was."

Corin nodded, his hand going out to shake John's before he headed back into the house. Cara threw herself into his arms as soon as he turned from closing the door.

"Corin. I was so afraid he'd hurt you."

"I'm fine, love. He did hit John, so he'll be facing charges on that. Now, where were we?"

"I have no idea." She went to turn, but he caught her back to him, wrapping her in his arms in a big hug before he kissed her.

She leaned back. "I could get used to this."

Corin let out a shout of laughter as she grinned, slipped from his arms and ran for the kitchen.

John stood in the observation room, Peter at his side, watching Tam move restlessly. He felt his jaw where Tam's fist had caught him and knew he'd have a bruise.

"Why did he come back, Dad?"

"That's what he won't say. I've had our best in there talking to him until he asked for a lawyer."

Peter shook his head. "He was always on the wild side. That's why I could never figure out Cara dating him."

"He hid what he did well, son. None of us knew what he was really like, unfortunately. He shouldn't have come back. I found outstanding charges against him, that are still valid. He'll be going away for a while. I have Jerry over at the judge's chambers right now working on warrants for his vehicle and his lodgings. He's been back three or four months but hasn't let anyone know."

Peter stared at his father. "That's almost when the trouble for Cara started."

John nodded. "It was. A bit after the first incident, but he could have very well have orchestrated that."

"I know and that scares me. We have no idea who all he's talked to. I haven't seen Beth back in town, either, but I heard she's been seen."

"So have I. We'll find her. She can't hide forever."

"But how much damage can she do in the mean while?" Peter walked away, leaving his father staring after him, acknowledging that he was right.

# Chapter 14

The next day, Corin snapped his measuring tape closed and set in on the shelf he was around.  He was almost finished with this remodel of a kitchen and then he would be moving on to another house.  He looked around, feeling someone watching him but not seeing anyone there.  He shrugged and bent to pick up the next shelf he needed to cut to length.

Hearing a movement behind him, he turned but not quick enough.  He was driven into the shelving, his ribs hitting hard.  He gave a shout of pain and tried to shove against his assailant but a blow to his back sent him to the floor.  He stopped feeling the kicks landing on him, doing his best to cover his face and head.  Finally his assailant stood back, breathing hard, before he pulled an envelope from his pocket with gloved hands, looking at it and then dropping it on Corin's crumpled body.

John came looking for Corin.  Corin had been working on a rental house John had bought and had asked him to stop by that day as he needed some decisions made. John stood for a moment outside, admiring the work Corin had put in and then walked through the door, heading for the living room and then through the bedrooms before he walked into the kitchen. A low cry was forced from his body and he was across the room and on his knees, his hands reaching for Corin.

"Corin? Can you hear me?"

Corin lay still. John saw the bruising on his arms and feared the worse, reaching for his phone to call for help.

"Corin, who did this to you? You need to wake up, lad, and tell me."

Pacing the Emergency Room, John worried about Cara, knowing that Peter had gone for her. Cara ran through the doors, not seeing him, heading for the clerk. A few words and she was through the door to where he knew Corin was. Peter stopped beside his father.

"Any word?"

John shook his head. "Not yet. It's too soon. Cara headed back so maybe we should to. Something beat him up pretty bad by the looks of it, using their boots. When will it end, Peter?"

Peter shook his head. "I have no idea. Tam's disappeared again and I heard he's with Beth. That's a combination I shudder to think about. But I haven't be able to confirm anything. And that is very unusual."

"It is. Keep working your sources. Head to the surrounding towns as well. I suspect they'll be hiding somewhere other than here. Here. This envelope was on his body. I haven't opened it yet. Get it to one of the techs." He looked up as Bruce and Emma entered, searching for Cara. "She's gone back, Bruce. We were just about to head back."

Bruce nodded. "Let us know what you can. Emma, here. I'll see if I can find out anything."

Cara stood at Corin's bedside, a hand on his arm, fear in her heart, as she watched the physician assessing him. The physician finally looked up, a reassuring look on his face.

"It's not as bad as it seems. However he fell, he fell in the right position to protect himself from a lot of damage. Bruising and lots of it. He may have a concussion but we won't know that until he wakes up." His eyes went to Corin. "And it looks as if that's exactly what he's doing."

Cara thanked him, her attention back on her beloved's face. She didn't hear John talking with the physician, or if she did, she ignored it. She felt an arm around her shoulder and her father's voice raised in prayer. She leaned against him and thanked him when he was done.

"How long, Dad? How long do we live like this?"

Bruce sighed, not having an answer for a question he knew she didn't really expect an answer to. "Soon, I pray, Cara. Soon. I'll go let your Mom know what said. One of us will be back here with you. The doctor said they'd be moving him to a room soon."

"They will be, Dad. I don't know how much more we can take. I thought he was gone when Peter came."

"I know you did, love. Perhaps it's time you two took the next step. You have our blessing if you do."

She looked up at her father, reading his face, before she nodded. "We've talked about that, Dad, just last night and set a date. We were going to talk to you and Mom tonight." Her words caught in a sob. "Now, it looks as if that's postponed too."

"When were you thinking?"

"About four weeks. We wanted to have it in the chapel at the camp and just open it up to friends who wanted to come. Nothing fancy at all."

"Sounds lovely, Cara. Talk to your mother and make your plans. We'll back whatever it is you two decide."

She kissed her father's cheek and hugged him. "Thank you, Dad. Not knowing what lies ahead has made it so difficult for us, but we don't want to waste any more time."

Bruce walked away from his daughter, stopping to lean against a wall to catch his breath and control his emotions. He felt a hand on his shoulder.

"Bruce? Is it Corin?" John's voice was quiet but full of worry.

"No, he's fine. Still unconscious but so fortunate that he wasn't hurt worse than he was." He paused. "No, it's something else. I need to talk to Emma first." He looked back at the room. "How do we end this, John? How do we keep them safe until we catch whoever it is? As time has gone by, it is more and more apparent that it's not Tam and

171

not Beth. He's all words unless he's changed. She doesn't have the character at all."

John nodded. "I agree with you. We're still searching for that family. We expanded our search to more areas. We've had some leads but nothing has panned out."

"You know, they used to allow camping on that property next to us. It was a well known fact. You just had to talk to the caretaker and get approval. I hear Ed is still alive, living in Mistletoe."

"Now, why didn't I know that?"

Bruce shrugged. "I thought you did."

"I guess I did years ago, but I never thought of that. Looks as if I have a trip to Mistletoe to make. Coming with me?"

Bruce nodded, a grim look covering his face. "Absolutely. It will be good to see Ed again and find out if he knows anything."

He looked up to see Emma approaching, a hand to her mouth in worry. "He's fine, Emma. Cara's with him." He nodded to John as he moved away. "This had been a crimp in their plans. They had planned to sit us down tonight and tell us they had set a date."

"Oh, wonderful. I think." Emma sounded confused for a moment and Bruce hugged her. "Is it a long ways off?"

"Four weeks, Cara said. They want simple and in the chapel."

"Oh, lovely. A fall wedding. Just what she has always wanted. Can I go in with them?" She nodded at the door.

"Sure. I was coming to get you any way."

"Is he really all right, Bruce?" Emma looked up at her husband, worry evident.

"He's badly bruised, has a concussion, but he's alive and was starting to stir when I left. Come on. Let me get you to our kids."

Emma stood for a moment, her eyes on her daughter before she moved forward, an arm going around her daughter. "Has he woken up yet, Cara?"

"Not quite, Mom. Who did this?"

"I don't know, love, but we'll find out."

"Everyone's been saying that for months, and we're not closer to where we need to be." Cara was frustrated, that much was clear. "It's to the point, Mom, I just want to leave, go somewhere else, and not let anyone know where I am."

"Don't do that, Cara. We need you here." Emma was distressed, Cara so upset she didn't realize how her words affected her mother. Emma's eyes were on Corin, seeing his eyes were open and on Cara, just listening to her talk. "Cara, you said you and Corin had set a date. How be we concentrate on that instead of what's been going on? You need to enjoy the next few weeks."

Cara finally nodded. "We did. We were to talk to you and Dad tonight. I have notes of what we want. I'll get them to you later. It's not fancy, Mom, just a simple ceremony with a tea afterwards. That's all we want." Her eyes dropped to Corin, seeing his love in his for her. "Corin, you're awake. Oh, sweetheart, who did this?"

"I don't know." Corin shifted to raise himself on the bed, nodding as she hit the button to raise the head of the bed. "I just heard a noise and then someone was on me. Did John show up in time?"

Cara shook her head. "No, he didn't. He found you." She frowned. "He muttered something about an envelope." She turned towards the door, not seeing him. "Mom, did he say anything to you?"

"No, he didn't and no, you're not heading out to find him. Your place is here."

Emma turned to see Bruce at the doorway, beckoning her to come. "I'll be right back. Now, neither of you go anywhere." She hadn't realized her words, but Cara frowned, her eyes going to Corin and seeing the mirth in his eyes.

"Did she really just say that? You in bed and all?"

Corin finally gave a low laugh. "She did, love. She's worried about you and is trying to protect you."

"I know, and I wish she wouldn't."

Corin reached for her hand, his fingers playing with her ring. "Did you really mean that, about moving away?"

"No, not really, I guess. I'm just frustrated, Corin. We're not really any further ahead. If we are, John's not saying." She bit at her lip. "I think it's time we started our own investigation."

"And how do you propose we do just that?"

She shrugged. "I don't know. Surely, we can start looking at things, reading old newspapers, looking at who I know and see what we can find out about them."

Corin nodded, and regretted it. "Let me think it over.  I have a friend, Blackie, who can help once we can give him names."

"That will work."  She turned as she heard quiet footsteps and the physician entered.

"You're awake, Corin. Good. How are you feeling?"

Corin groaned. "How am I supposed to feel?  I feel like I've been run over by a large truck.  Isn't that the way it's supposed to be?"

The physician laughed, finished his examination, and then stood back.  "I'd like to admit you overnight but somehow I don't think you'll agree.  I'll release you as long as you have someone with you all night."  He wrote out a prescription and handed it to Cara.  "Here's some pain medications.  I'd like to see you back here in three days.  I want to check you over then."  He walked away, leaving Corin staring after him.

"Did he just say I can leave?"

She nodded.  "Let me go get Dad to help you.  You can't manage on your own."  She went to move away, but his hand stopped her and she looked down at him.

"Cara, never ever doubt that you are a beautiful, wonderful, compassionate woman that I love deeply.  I heard what you said to your Mom.  We'll fight this through together, both of us."  He watched until she finally nodded, his hand moving to her cheek before he raised himself to kiss her.  "Now, let's get me out of here so we can go make plans.  I'm not sure about the four weeks though."  A glint of mischief and love sparkled in his eyes as she stared, open mouthed at first, and then turned to find her father.

# *Chapter 15*

*A* week later, Corin stood in the chapel of the camp, nerves making him shake as he waited beside Nigel. After what had happened, they decided not to wait for the four weeks. Emma and Bruce had asked them that, why the wait? They both remembered how it was to be young and in love. They also knew, with what these two were going through, they needed that support for each other that being a married couple would bring.

Nigel elbowed Corin slightly, bringing him back to the present and making him turn slightly, his breath caught as he saw his bride, in a simple lace covered dress, her hair loose and under a lace veil. Her love for him shone as she got closer and reached for his hand.

Later that day, they stood, his arm around her, as they watched their friends and family mingle, laughter the order of the day. She looked up at him, a frown in place.

"Cara? Why the frown?"

She shrugged. "I don't know, Corin, but I think us taking this step has just changed everything. That what we faced in the past will be nothing like we will face. Do you remember our discussion about standing on the edge of a cliff, not knowing if we were safe or not?"

He nodded. "I do, but remember that we are not alone in that. God has us and if we fall, His hand will catch us and shelter us."

She agreed, a sigh still escaping her. "I know. It doesn't make it easier though. Sometimes it's so hard to trust." She leaned against him.

He hugged her tighter. "I know, love. It is hard. I always picture God's hand under us. A friend has a saying or a prayer really that she uses for friends going through some hard stuff. It goes something like this: I pray a band of angels around you, God's hand underneath you, the blood of Jesus over top of you, and the Comforter within you. She's prayed it for me and it really does work. She doesn't need to know what's happening, she'll just get a sense that someone needs prayer."

"That is so wonderful, Corin. I'd like to meet her some day."

"And some day, I'll introduce you to her. She's a busy lady, working and involved in her church. She would have been here today, but had another commitment."

"Oh, I'd like that." She turned as Nigel approached them and she reached to hug her brother.

Nigel hugged his sister a little tighter and held on a little longer than he normally would have. He knew without her saying anything that their relationship had entered a new phase, that he no longer was responsible for her, but that didn't mean he wouldn't be looking out for her.

Corin watched with compassion the siblings, then reached to hug Nigel himself, finally finding himself a brother. An only child, he had always wanted siblings, but that had not been God's plan, his parents explained. They had accepted that, turning to working in a mission in their home town and traveling once a year overseas for a few weeks. They were here somewhere, he knew. He had spent time with them and they had fallen in love with his bride.

Two weeks later, Cara looked up as Corin set samples of wood flooring on her desk. She had taken over a corner of his office space, but knew eventually she'd have to find room of her own. They were already talking of finding office space down town, where they would be more readily accessible to their clients.

"I think these are what you asked for, love. Are they?"

Cara looked them over. "Perfect." She sat back, knowing something else was on his mind. "Corin, did John talk to you by chance?"

He nodded. "He did. He finally tracked down the family. He didn't give a name but he said they were not connected to you, your family or the camp in any way. They were moving across the country and had decided to make it a vacation for their kids."

She nodded, sadness filling her. "That's so wrong. So sad. It shouldn't have happened. Now what?"

"Now what, he starts looking more at people here in town. He says he's sure someone knows something. Tam seems to be around more and John thinks he's been blackmailing someone over the years and that the person has likely balked at paying, now that the bodies are found."

"I can see that, but Tam is the type of person who won't give up.  I know that."

Corin hugged her, knowing the trauma she had suffered because of him.  They had had many a talk over the past few months, Cara telling more and more what it had been like for her near the end of her friendship with both Tam and Beth.  "I am so glad you managed to get away from him."

"So am I."  She looked at the clock.  "What did you want for dinner?"

"How be I take my bride out for a meal?"  He grinned as she shook a finger at him before sneaking some kisses.

Her face rosy, she walked away, confident finally in who she was and in his love.

Corin watched her leave, and then turned to a call he had to make.  John had left a voice mail for him, that he hadn't gotten a chance to return.  He walked through the house to the backyard as he waited.

"John?  It's Corin.  You had called earlier."

John sounded distracted.  "I did, Corin. Where's Cara?"

"In the house. We're planning on going out to dinner."

'No!" John's voice was forceful enough it stopped Corin in his tracks.

"Why not?"

"Because we just had another package delivered. It goes with that letter that was left on you that day, the one I told you about. The one that warned judgement was coming for you both."

"I remember, but what about it?" Corin turned to face Cara, who had approached him, a frown on her face as she listened to his side of the conversation, drawing her over to him so she could listen to.

"The package held another doll. This time it had real blood on it, Corin. The tech says animal."

Cara drew a deep breath, then steeled herself. "What did the letter with it say, John?"

"Cara, you're there. Good." He sighed and they heard his frustration. "There was no letter. No picture. Just the doll. The package was addressed to you, Cara, in your married name. Someone knows you've married, and where you're living."

"Okay. So, now what? I'm not running and hiding, you can forget that."

John gave a bark of laughter. "Didn't think you would, Cara. That's not who you are." They could hear him talking to someone before he came back to them. "I'm having to run. Stay home tonight, please? I'll be by later."

She frowned as Corin pocketed his phone, then hugged her. "I was so looking forward to dinner out tonight."

"I know, love. So was I. Now, which one of us is cooking?" He dodged the elbow she levered at him.

"I'm suddenly not that hungry, Corin. What do you want?"

He shrugged as he turned them back to the house, pausing as he frowned. Something was off. He suddenly ran back down the yard, pulling Cara with him, his phone out as he frantically called for help. He swept her into his arms and to the ground as an explosion racketed through the air, sending debris falling, some of it bouncing off his back. He raised up, his eyes on Cara, seeing the fright in them and the anger.

"Did someone just blow up our house, Corin?"

He nodded as he helped her to sit up, his arm tight around her as he searched for his phone. He looked down to see it clutched in her hand. "How'd you get my phone?"

She stared at it. "I have no idea. I think I must have taken it from you when you threw us to the ground." She stared at again, then thrust it at him, hearing John's voice yelling over it. "Here. You talk to him." She stared at the house they were just starting to make a home, destroyed now, lying in a pile of rubble, flames flickering as they gathered ground. She shuddered. "It had been so close, Corin. If you hadn't come out to talk to John and if I hadn't come to find you, we would have been in there."

He nodded, his thoughts echoing hers. "God led us there, Cara love. He had me come outside. I had no intention of doing that, you know. Something compelled me outside. I didn't want you to overhear my conversation."

She hugged him, realizing just how close they had come. Her thoughts shifted, anger starting to burn inside her. God, thank you. You've protected us once again. But when will it end? How much more danger we will have to face? Lost in her thoughts, still cradled against Corin as they sat staring at the house, she didn't hear John's yells from the front of the house, didn't see him shielding his face from the smoke, seeking to find them, finally seeing them and running towards them, Peter on his heels.

John dropped to a crouch in front of them, his hands reaching out to their shoulders.

"You're alive. Thank God! I thought the worst before I saw you." He adjusted his stance, his face turning towards the house, nodding as Peter spoke in a low voice before heading back around to the front, where the sirens had stopped, but red and blue emergency lights lit up the darkening sky.

"Corin?" John's voice finally reached him. "Are you two all right?" John looked up as he heard the paramedics approaching.

Corin finally released Cara to their care, shrugging them off until Cara refused to be seen unless he was. He waited impatiently for them to assess them.

John walked back towards them, his voice low as he talked to an officer, who nodded and headed down the yard, searching for any evidence. John knew Bruce and Emma were being kept at the roadblock and had sent word the young couple were fine. They had been in touch with Nigel, who had been away on a trip. He had taken an interest in the mission Corin's parents were involved with.

Corin walked towards him, his body turning as he stopped so he could watch Cara where she sat, having a cut on her arm dressed, under protest he noticed with a small grin.

"John? What happened? You told us to stay home because it wasn't safe, and then the house explodes."

"I know, Corin, I know. The word I had and that we were trying to verify was that you two were a target, that something was planned for tonight. The word we had was that you were going out for dinner and you would be hit then."

Corin's hand froze as he raised it to his face. "That was a spur of the moment decision, John. We had no plans of doing that. I just wanted a meal out with my bride, to save us from cooking. Then you called and we changed our minds." He spun, staring at the house. "It's too late now, but do you suppose someone had put in a listening device?"

John nodded. "That's possible, but you know we've been going over your house on a regular basis, just for that kind of equipment. Unless someone is listening in from outside."

He was puzzled. "I'll have to wait for the arson investigator's report but this was deliberate, Corin. I have no doubt of that." He turned as Cara approached, reaching for Corin's hand. "Cara, you're not hurt too bad?"

She shook her head. "Can we leave? I need to see Mom and Dad."

"We can. Here, let's get you over to your neighbour's yard and you can walk out through there."

Cara paused, her eyes looking at first one house and then the one on the other side. "Have they been damaged?"

"They'll be looked at, but I don't think so. From what I was told, the force of the explosion went up, not out. That's a saving factor for the homes."

Corin studied the debris and realized what seemed off to him. "That's weird, John. Why would they do that?"

John shrugged. "A question we'll ask when we find them. Unless Tam and Beth have taken up making explosives or know someone who does, it can't be them." He held up a hand. "I'm not discounting them, don't worry."

Cara ran for her mother when she saw her, seeing tears on her face. Hugged tight, she felt her father's arms come around them and knew he was crying too. It had been too close, she thought.

Emma turned to Corin, finally, sweeping him into a hug that she didn't want to end. Bruce stood, a hand out for Corin, before he too hugged him.

"Thank you, Corin. Your actions, I understand, kept you both alive."

Corin shrugged, genuinely puzzled by why he had left the house. "I don't normally go outside to take phone calls. Something made me."

"God, Corin. That's the only explanation. He moves us to do things we don't understand, keeping us safe, or alerting us to something wrong. That's what He did. Because you were obedient and listened to that nudge, you survived."

Corin nodded, his face pale, dirt marking it and streaking his clothes. He wrapped his arms around Cara as they stood, eyes on their home, not sure what they would do now.

"We've talked, Cara. You and Corin have the pick of whatever cabin you want until you decide what you want to do." Bruce held up a hand as Corin went to protest. "Corin, you're family. This is what we do as family. It's that or the house." Bruce subtly nodded at Cara.

Corin realized the out Bruce was giving them. "I don't know, Cara. Too many cabins to choose from."

She sighed. "I know. I think Peace would be the one. We need that in our lives right now, and it's the first one near the house. The security system from the house shows it and we can add security to it."

Bruce approved her choice, but didn't say anything. It was a decision the couple had to make, as a couple, without any interference from her parents. Emma caught his eye and nodded.

"Let's get you two home then. We'll need to find some clothes for you two, though."

"I still have some at the house, Mom, some I hadn't really decided if I wanted to keep. And Corin always has a duffle bag packed in the truck, just in case he needs to change to meet a client."

"Good planning, you two." Bruce turned away, then turned back. "Corin, your truck?"

Corin grimaced. "John said it was destroyed. All my records and plans are gone from there as well as in the house." He turned Cara away. "I think it's time we set up an office somewhere, some place we can wire up for security as much as we can. We had planned that in the future, not just yet."

Bruce nodded. "I agree. For now, there's the workshop in the garage you can set up in." He stopped, his hand reaching out stop Corin's forward motion. "Did you save anything to an internet program?"

Corin stopped, wonder coming to him. "I had forgotten all about that. Yes, I have. Everything. I hadn't but something in the last week prompted me to do just that." He looked down at Cara, seeing her white face, the dark circles under her eyes, the dirt and stress marking her beauty. "I saved Cara's as well." She looked up, a smile on her face that didn't reach her eyes.

"Thank you, love. We talked about it and I meant to."

An hour later, fed with toast and tea, Corin gently helped Cara into the shower and then walked away to wait. He needed to make some decisions and needed Cara to help make those. They could no longer go on as they were. He felt that now he had to go on the offensive, just as Cara had wanted. He turned as he heard the shower shut off and walked back to the bedroom, finding Cara in her nightwear, just standing, tears streaming down her face.

"Ah, Cara, love. Come here." Corin wrapped her in his arms before turning her into the bedroom and making her lie down, covering her with the blankets and laying down beside her, his arms reaching for her, his lips speaking prayers that he didn't hear, but Cara did and relaxed, finally falling asleep, feeling safe for the first time in hours.

Corin rose once he felt confident Cara wouldn't awake and heading for the living room, took the laptop Bruce had loaned him, pulling up his email and sending off an quick email to his friend, asking if they could meet, preferably here in town. The response was quick. Both Blackie and his father would be there in the morning. Corin sent off his address with a quick thanks.

He felt a hand on his neck and tilted his head back. Cara stood there, uncertainty in her stance. He drew her down with him and they cuddled together, neither saying a word, just thankful they were there.

"What now, Corin? You can't work until the insurance comes through with money for tools."

He shrugged. "I can get some and then submit the bills. I'll buy what I absolutely need and then go from there." His chin rested on her head. "But what about you? You've lost all your research material, your books, your samples."

"I know. I can get them again. I just hate this. Hate that we have to start all over. And why? Who's after us? Who wants to hurt us this badly?"

Corin sighed, knowing that she was right. "I have no idea, love. Blackie and his dad are heading our way tomorrow morning. We'll sit down with them and see what they can do for us. Samuel's good at working through puzzles and finding answers. He had a natural gift for that, a God-given one I've heard said. Blackie does too." He gave a small laugh and she tilted her head to look at him. "Sorry, love. Blackie went through an adventure as he called it, before he married Julia, one that almost killed him." He reached for his phone, sending off a quick message to Blackie. "I should have him bring Julia with him. She'll be a good person for you to talk to."

"That would be wonderful, Corin, to talk to someone who knows what this is like. None of our friends do." Her head went back down and she was silent.

He could feel her body getting heavier as she slipped away to sleep and didn't have the heart to awaken her. He reached for the blanket Emma had set on the back of the couch and shook it out, covering Cara.

He rose in the early morning, gathering his wife into his arms and carrying her back through to the bedroom, tucking her up to continue her sleep. He watched as she turned, her hand reaching for his pillow as she always did, a soft sigh coming from her. He reached over and kissed her temple, then straightened back up. Enough was enough, he thought. Whoever it was had been winning so far. That was over, as far as he was concerned. He headed back for the kitchen, reaching for the coffee pot. It was only four in the morning, and it was going to be a long day, he already knew. The stress of it would tire them both out.

He reached for a pad of paper and a pen, stopping as he saw the Bible laying there. Instead of the pen, he reached for that Book, immersing himself in verses about being strong, being of good courage, of standing on the brink of trouble, of finding the high tower, and of hiding in God's hands. He sat back, finally reaching for the coffee and the pen and paper.

Listing everyone he could think of that he knew and that Cara knew, he saw the list was long. He didn't realize he knew that many people. But someone wasn't there, he realized. He took a second paper, and listed family, knowing Samuel would want their names. It was difficult, this list, but so necessary. He knew John would have investigated them, but he was too close, Corin thought. He needed fresh eyes.

He looked up as he heard the shower and rose, putting on the kettle for Cara's tea and reaching into the fridge for the breakfast items Emma had left, even while insisting they come to the house for that meal. He knew Cara wouldn't be ready at that time of the morning to face her parents.

Cara stood for a moment before heading for Corin's open arms. She stood, feeling safe, wanted, loved, before she peeked over his arm at the counter.

"What are you making, love?"

"Breakfast." He grinned as he turned back to his meal preparations. "Just an omelet and toast. I don't think you're too hungry."

She shook her head as she reached for the tea he had prepared for her. "I'm not. Corin, what are we to do?"

"For now, we eat. Then we talk." He moved his papers off the table to the counter. "I've been making some lists but before I did that, I searched for verses to help. Here's my list."

She reached for the paper, her eyes thanking him. "This is good, Corin. We need to make a copy so we both have one. That way we can look at it any time we need to. God will not let this continue much longer, that I'm sure of."

"No, he won't. It's coming to a head, love, and soon. That much I can sense. I just don't who it is, that's the thing." He reached for her hand as he asked the blessing on their food.

She ate mechanically, not really tasting what he had prepared, her thoughts on who it could be. An idea was gelling, and she didn't like it one bit.

"Corin, what if it's someone close to us, someone we trust implicitly? Is that possible?"

He nodded. "I've already thought of that." He sorted through his papers, handing her the one list. "Look this over." He nudged the pen closer to her with a tanned forefinger. "Add to it. I don't think I got everyone. I want you to add to what I've listed." He ate in silence as she read the list, then pulled over the pen and began adding names.

She read back through the list, her eyes hesitating at a name. "You've listed everyone, haven't you?"

"We have to, love. Blackie will search them and let us know if we need to be concerned. He doesn't know them, so he has nothing to hinder his search."

She nodded. "I guess. It just feels like we're violating their privacy, but I guess we're not. Not after what whoever it is has done to us."

"We're not, not really, Cara. John has likely looked into most of these people."

She sighed. " I know but there are names here I didn't give him. It wasn't deliberate. I just didn't think of them at the time."

"And he'll understand. Now, I can tell you've zeroed in on one." He watched with compassion as she nodded.

"I have, and I don't like it one bit." She gave him the name and he started, knowing that was who he had questioned. "You're not surprised, are you?"

He sighed himself, knowing he had to confess. "Not really. That name has a big question mark for me as well." He looked at the clock. "Blackie said they'd be here about 9:30. That gives us a couple of hours to start making some lists of the essentials."

She nodded as she rose and cleared the table, washing the dishes and leaving them to drain as Corin cleared up the cooking mess. As he reached for the dish cloth, he paused, his eyes on her face, before he kissed her.

Her hand on his cheek, she leaned back. "Hmm. I sort of like having you around." She grinned as he hugged her. "Now, where's the paper and pens? I really don't want to do this, you know."

Corin laughed as he headed for the desk in the corner, picking up the paper, but his hand stilling as he did so. He lifted the photo from the wall and turned to her, to find her watching him

"Corin? What now?"

"This picture. I know we placed it here, but I just don't know. There's something off about it." He handed her to her as she stopped beside him.

She studied it. "There is. This isn't the same picture we put there. I know it isn't. There's an extra person in this one. Now who changed this?"

"Who's the person?" Corin knew she had the name on her lips to tell him.

"It's a cousin, cousin Joseph. He's from Dad's side. He resented the fact that Mom and Dad started this camp on land they inherited. He always thought the land should have been sold and the money divided. He never forgave them and left about fourteen years ago. I had almost forgotten him. Now that I see him again, I can remember the arguments that went on. They were brutal. He became vicious." She raised her eyes to him. "He's one name not on the list. We need to add him and get his name to John."

"John is to come out this afternoon, just to go over last night with us." He turned, heading back for the table. "We'll let Blackie take that with him. It will help."

An hour later, Cara sat back from her lists, frustrated at having to replace everything she owned. She was grateful neither one of them had been hurt, but it didn't make it any easier, she thought. Corin looked up with a smile, then bent his head back over his tool list. It was getting lengthy, he knew. First thing would be shopping for vehicles and that he never enjoyed.

Cara stood for a moment, hesitating about where she needed to be. Her feet carried her back to the bedroom and the Bible she had there. She pulled out her phone, finding the photo she had taken of Corin's list of verses. She needed this time with God, to get her perspective back.

Corin finally came looking for her, knowing it was soon time for Blackie to arrive. He stood for a moment, watching as she read, quiet confidence and peace surrounding her. She had worked through her fear and made the determination, that come what may, she would face this person and defeat them, even if it meant her death, and that was a good possibility. She would not tell Corin of her determination, but he would know, just from reading her. That she couldn't prevent.

Cara looked up as Corin spoke, then rose, going towards him. "They're here?"

"Soon, love. Your Mom stopped by. She left some more food and some clothes for both of us. She was out shopping as soon as the stores opened apparently. She said the merchants opened early for her, given who she was shopping for."

"That's so nice of them. That's what a small town is like." She paused as she heard the sound of footsteps.

Corin headed for the door, opening it to Blackie and his father, Samuel. He introduced Cara to them and then looked around Blackie, not seeing anyone else. "Julia didn't come?"

Blackie shook his head. "She already had a commitment she couldn't get out of. She'll come next time. Now, where can we sit?"

"The kitchen." Cara pointed it out. "It's close to the coffee, tea, and the treats I know Mom brought over. I just wish it was in our own home."

Blackie had been looking around. "This is nice. The cabin name is Peace?" When she nodded, he continued. "I like that. Who designed the interior?" He looked at them as Corin laughed and Cara blushed.

"Cara did, and she won't admit it on her own."

Blackie looked at her and then at his father, who nodded.

"Cara, we're updating homes and apartments that we own and are renting or selling to low-income families, where we can legally sell them.  The charter for Mistletoe is specific enough that sometimes we can't. Would you be willing to work for us?  Come over and start going through them and then giving us your designs, overseeing the progress?"  Samuel knew he was almost begging, but he wanted her to work for them.

She finally nodded. "I will, thank you. It will take a while though to get my supplies to where I need them."

"Give me a list.  I have contacts and will get that filled for you.  Corin, your tools - let me have that list.  And vehicles.  We can look after that for you."

Corin shook Samuel's hand as Cara watched in shock.  He would explain afterwards why and how they would do this.

Samuel finally sat back, his mind racing with the information they had given him. "We'll work on it, Corin. We'll make it a priority.  I'll put everyone on it. Hopefully in twenty-four hours, we'll have some kind of an answer.  I know that seems like a long time, given what you're facing, but we'll get you through this."

The father and son finally walked away, leaving the young couple staring at one another, shocked with the help offered them.

"Corin, they can't do that."

"Cara, love, they can and will. Samuel has millions of dollars at his control, something he didn't know he had. It all goes back to the town of Mistletoe. Someday, we'll tell you that story. I want you to meet Julia. You'll like her, I know."

He turned as a tap came to the door, opening it to John. John studied the two in front of them, sensing something different about them.

"What do you two go and do?" John looked between them.

"Nothing that you need to be concerned about. A friend and his father dropped by today, that's all." Corin was being deliberately vague, and John knew that well.

John sighed. "I just wish you'd let us do the investigating."

"That's worked out so well, John, now hasn't it?" Cara's words had a bite to them, one that took John by surprise. He had not heard that in her voice ever before.

"Cara? You know we're doing everything we can to find the people responsible and to keep you safe."

"Well, that certainly didn't work out so well last night. Now, you're here. What is the update?" Cara refused to back down, refused to give in to his plea. She was done with being nice, she decided.

"It was a bomb placed in the crawl space, centred under the house. It took the arson investigator a while to find the spot, but his dog did. There wasn't much left for them to find, but he did say it was a homemade device from what he could see."

"Great. Someone goes on the internet, finds out how to build a bomb, and plants it in our house." Cara paced, Corin leaning against the wall watching her, seeing John's discomfort at her words.

"Unfortunately, I think you're right, Cara. There was nothing left that we could use to identify the person."

"That seems too odd, John. That's what you're always saying about this. Why?"

John stepped back, not liking what he was hearing. "I see. I guess I'll be on my way, then, Cara. When you want to talk to me, you'll know where to find me. I'll be in touch with more information as we get it." He turned and walked away, frustrated that this wasn't over and frustrated that Cara no longer seemed to trust him. Given what had happened, he couldn't say that he blamed her.

Corin watched as Cara continued to pace. "That wasn't really fair to John, love."

"I know, but maybe it will make him look harder. There has to be something out there we can find and use. What are we missing?"

He wrapped her in his arms as she stopped in front of him, waiting for her to relax. "I don't know, but I'm sure Blackie will come up with something for us."

"I still can't believe they want me to work for them. I never expected that." Her eyes lit up with excitement at the thought.

"If Samuel asked it, then he means it. He also means it about our lists and for vehicles. It wouldn't surprise me to see a vehicle for each of us here today. He was asking some light questions there, in case you missed it, light in the sense that he didn't want us to know what he was after."

"I didn't," Cara replied. "I just didn't grasp that's what he was after. Did you?"

"Not at first. Not until he said that. And he will do it, you know."

"We can't accept them."

"Unfortunately, whether we want to or not, we will have to. He would be really hurt if we didn't." He turned her in his arms and gently shoved her towards the door. "Now, let's lock up and go see what your mother has planned for us."

Cara groaned. "I don't want to know, thank you very much."

He laughed as he pulled the door closed and tried it. "It's not that bad, is it?"

She shook her head. "You don't know Mom when she's on a mission, and she will be with this."

"No. Your Dad talked to me last night. Your Mom understands that this is different, that we will make choices based on what we want. She's fine with that. Don't be afraid to speak up. If you don't, I will. Understood?"

She nodded as she lifted her eyes. "I can feel someone watching us, Corin. But who?"

He looked around, having the same feeling. "I don't know, love, but let's get you inside the house." He hurried her forward to the house.

Bruce looked up in surprise at the speed they enter the house, a frown appearing as

Corin shook his head and pointed down the hall. He greeted his daughter and then asked Corin if he could talk with him, something about a new building they were thinking of adding.

Corin agreed, after making sure Cara was fine. He hated not having her with him, but he knew he had to leave her, just so he could talk with Bruce.

Bruce quietly shut the door behind Corin and pointed to the easy chairs near the fireplace.

"What's wrong, Corin? I could see it in your faces."

"We're being watched again, Bruce. I just don't know who or where they were."

Bruce nodded. "Andy, the security guard we hired, has seen traces of people around where they shouldn't be. He hasn't caught anyone yet though."

Corin leaned back, sighing. "I want this over yesterday, Bruce. I want Cara safe."

"So do we. What would you suggest?"

Corin spoke rapidly, outlining the plan he had come up with during the night. Bruce stared at him, knowing the danger he would be in, but wondering if it would be the only way to catch the culprit. "I don't like the danger, Corin. Nor the fact you'd be putting yourself out there."

"I know. I can't put Cara out there. But that will happen. I just don't know what to do."

Bruce thought it through. "Leave it with me for a day or two. This is something you and I need to pray over. It will be our ladies at risk, and we want to minimize that as much as we can."

Corin agreed, finally glad to have someone agree with him. "I have a name, though, that Cara came up with." He hesitated to give it, knowing the close relationship Bruce shared. "It's John's other brother."

Bruce stared at him, shock on his face. "Jeremy? He's been gone from here for years."

"How many years exactly, Bruce? He would have known what the culprit knows."

Bruce sat back, shocked and saddened. "I know. Fourteen years, Corin. He was here when that family was murdered. He always scraped along the edge. We were never sure if he slipped over into crime or not. We suspected but could never prove anything."

"I asked Blackie to look into him." Corin held up a hand as Bruce opened his mouth. "Blackie and his father will keep it confidential unless we ask them to pass on the information. And they will amass a multitude of information. We gave them a list of names and they'll research every one as far as they can. And they're good at what they do."

Bruce finally nodded. "I understand why you went that route. John would feel obligated to investigate but he would be too close. And you don't have any evidence to ask another force to investigate Jeremy."

"That's what we decided." He rose and then turned. "I know without asking you won't tell Emma. That's a given for now."

Bruce had also risen. "No, I won't. No need to worry her yet. Let's head out and see what the women have decided to do."

Cara turned to Corin later that afternoon. "How did the talk with Dad go?"

"It went well. He thinks we may be on to something but that we'll need to wait for Blackie to get back to us." He set his mug down on the table. "I have a feeling it's not going to be that long a wait."

"I don't think it will be either. It has that feeling, doesn't it?" She shivered, not from cold but from fear. "If it is Jeremy, where has he been and where is he now? He would know this property well. He spent a lot of time on it." She stopped, hit by a sudden thought. "Corin! Our home! That was his!"

"It was? I didn't know that. It wasn't him that I bought it from."

"No, it's changed hands many times over the last few years. People had said it was haunted, but I wonder if it was Jeremy all along."

"It likely was. We'll have to wait and see." He looked at the clock. "It's Sunday tomorrow, Cara. Be prepared to be questioned and hugged and loved on at church, and to be offered the moon." He grinned at the expression on her face.

## Chapter 16

*T*hree days later, Blackie came looking for Corin, worry on his face. He and his father were confident they had found their man, John's brother, Jeremy. But just how much did John play in this? That was the question they couldn't answer, not yet anyway.

Cara stood back from the door, her hand extended to usher Blackie in.

"Come in, Blackie. Corin had to run an errand, but he should be back in the next few minutes. Can I get you a tea or coffee?"

"Tea would great, if it's no trouble." He slid into a seat at the kitchen table, taking a look once more around the cabin, liking what he saw. "Dad's excited to have you working on our projects. In fact, he sent a folder for you of the first one he'd like you to tackle. It's for a friend, so he wants to spare no expense."

Cara set their mugs down and reached for the folder, flipping it open, her eyes studying each photo and then the details of what the house was about. "Your Dad loves his research, doesn't he?  This is great.  I already have some ideas."

"That's wonderful, Cara."  He looked up as the back door opened and Corin walked in, dropping his boots on a tray and then greeting Cara before filling a mug with coffee and sliding into a chair beside her.

"Blackie?  I didn't expect you to make the trip. I thought you'd call."

Blackie shook his head.  "This is too sensitive to call or send by email.  We've found your culprit."  He watched as the couple turned to one another and then to him. "You were right, Cara.  Corin, so were you. Both of you."

"Both of us?  How can that be?"

"Somehow, Jeremy has connected with Beth's father.  They knew each other from town, from what we discovered, went their separate ways but connected again over the last year.  Did you know that Beth's father was like that, Cara?"

Cara shook her head.  "He never showed that side of him.  He did have a temper but it never was directed towards his family. He loved them. Beth always was his little girl." Her voice died away at a thought.

"That's why.  He blames me for what happened, for her leaving town with Tam. Is that it?"

"Part we think.  We've tracked down a man from their past, who was a young man at the time.  He has confirmed both Jeremy and Edward were heavily involved in smuggling in drugs and stolen artifacts and stolen jewelry.  We suspect the property next door was used as a drop site and that the family that died was simply in the wrong place at the wrong time.  Their car has never been found, but there was a car found around that time, burned and with the VIN destroyed.  That was likely theirs."

Cara shivered, rubbing her hands up and down her arms, distress of her face. Corin's arm wrapped around her and pulled her close. "How does this help us, Blackie?"

"I've talked to another friend of mine, who is a police officer.  He's offered to look into it, with his supervisor's blessing, I might add.  They both think John is too close to this, and we don't want to miss anything.  Simon's supervisor is reaching out to John today, to talk to him, giving him the information we have found.  John may or may not come and talk to you.  We'd prefer that you didn't say anything to him.  Let them work it through. These two people are nasty.  It's no wonder you two have been haunted like you have been.  The supervisor is surprised you haven't been hurt worse or even killed."

"They're playing with us, Blackie, like a cat toying with a mouse.  Just waiting for the right time.  Somehow, I don't think it's that far off."

Blackie shook his head.  "No, I don't think it is.  It's been what, you said, five or six months now since you found the bodies?"  At their nod, he continued, "Then, whatever happens will likely happen in the next couple of weeks.  That much we've head from scuttlebutt around your town."

"And how did you hear that?"

"A friend came in and talked to people.  You wouldn't know him, though.  He keeps a pretty low profile when he needs to."  Blackie grinned at the frown Cara shot him.  "Hopefully, it will be over soon, Cara, and you can get on with your life.  Believe me when I say, I know what you're feeling. Julia and I went through something horrible last December, something I would not want anyone else to go through. We survived, with God's help, and so will you.  Corin, it's getting to the point now that it will be very dangerous for both of you.  I don't need to tell you that.  If what you've gone through hasn't worked, hasn't killed you, then they will up the activity and try to get to you. Stay together as much as you can. Dad's arranging for three of his security team to head over here today."

"Security? Does he think that necessary?" Corin was surprised.

"He does. These three men are the best of the best and will be with you, one on duty at all times, right outside here. They also have dogs they are bringing in as well. We need you two to stay here as much as possible, and to keep others away from you. If we have to, Dad can make arrangements to get you to a safe house until we find these men."

"Somehow, I don't think we'd make it to a safe house, Blackie. Not with how we're being watching. Bruce said the security guard he's had here during the day has seen traces of people where they shouldn't be." Corin heard Cara's soft gasp and tightened his arm on her. "I would suggest your fellows talk to him. His name's Andy. And talk to Bruce."

"Dad has already done that today. He was calling him as I left. If we have to, we'll move your parents and brother away for safety, Cara."

"They won't go, Blackie.  I know that."

Blackie sighed.  "About what I thought you'd say."  He finally stood, his eyes on the two.  "Stay safe.  We'll working it through. Don't open the door to anyone unless they can prove who they are and they're from us."

Corin slid back into his chair after closing the door and locking it behind Blackie, reaching for Cara's hands.  He didn't say anything at first, just turned her rings on her finger.  She touched his ring and then looked up.

"This is is, isn't it, Corin?  The end is near, isn't it?"

He nodded, a sober expression of his face.  "It is, love.  This is where we'll need to trust God so much.  We won't get through it without him.  I love you so much.  I wish I could take this from you and keep you from going through the next few days."

She shook her head, a trembling smile on her lips even as she fought tears.  "You're so strong, Corin, so strong and courageous.  I can't let you take this from me. It won't work that way.  They have to be stopped and this is the only way, to go forward.  Now, we have plans to make, you and I.  We need to decide what we're going to do about a home.  While cozy, this cabin is too small. Unless we find that office space you want in town."

"I like that idea better and better, Cara. That way, we don't have clients coming to our home. It stays ours, our sanctuary. Especially if at some time in the future God blesses us with a family, we don't want strangers in and out."

Cara had blushed at that, but agreed. "I think so too." She reached for the laptop, finding the real estate section she wanted. "These are buildings that are for rent or sale. Which would you prefer?"

"To buy, if we can swing it. That way, it's ours and we can fix it the way we want to." He paused her hand. "Wait. That one. It has an apartment above it. That would work for now, wouldn't it? We could live there while we're rebuilding, if that's what we want to do."

"I'm not sure I can ever go back there, Corin. Knowing that a family member tried to kill us there?" She shuddered at the thought.

He hugged her tight to him. "I know. I feel the same. If you hadn't come out to look for me, I would have lost you."

She nodded, even as she flicked through the listings, not seeing another one she liked. "We can contact Bonnie. She's the agent. This place has been for sale for a long time." She paused, a thought crossing her mind. "I'm not sure who owns it now."

"We'll pass it on to Blackie. He'll find out for us." He sat back, his eyes on the wall across from him, not seeing what he was looking at. "We need to really pray for safety, love. It's going to get brutal. That's what I'm feeling."

"I know." Her head dropped to her folded arms. She dozed off, Corin finally scooping her into his arms before he carried her through to the bedroom and tucked her under a blanket.

Cara finally rose, her thoughts disoriented for a moment, pausing as she heard voices from the other room. She stood for a moment, watching Corin talking to a man she didn't know, but recognized as likely one of the security guards Blackie had told them about.

Corin turned, reaching out a hand, introducing her to the man, who shook her hand and then left shortly afterwards. Cara stood, clutching Corin's hand, not really believing they were at that point.

"It's true, love. We have security now with us at all times."

"I hate this, Corin." She pulled free and started to pace. Corin sat on the arm of the couch, his eyes watching her movement, knowing he had to let her vent. "Why? What did I ever do?"

"Let Tam walk away from you? Let Beth go with Tam? That's her father's motivation. As to Jeremy, I don't know. Unless it's because you were there when the bodies were found. Unless......". His voice died away, a horrible thought coming to him.

She spun, her eyes on his face, a frown on her. "Unless what?"

"Did you hear or see anything all those years ago, something so insignificant that you really brushed past it, but Jeremy would think you had remembered? That would be his motivation. Thinking you could implicate him in the murders."

She thought back. "I really don't remember, Corin. And I've gone back over my diaries from that year. I didn't see any reference to anything at all." She thought again, then shook her head. "He's after me for nothing at all."

It was Corin's turn to shake his head. "There has to be something. Something about that cabin that you would have noticed and thought off, but not worried enough about to bring to anyone's attention."

She had begun to pace again as he spoke, then spun, fright on her face. "Oh, no! There was! I had forgotten all about it. Oh, Corin! What did I do?"

He reached for her, drawing her to him, holding her as she sobbed, murmuring words of comfort. He finally sat on the couch, drawing her down onto his lap and wrapping his arms tight around her as she continued to sob. Her sobs finally eased and she lay still against him.

"What did you remember?"

"I saw blood on the steps but thought it was an animal's blood. We've had that in other cabins. I didn't see any in the cabin, but I remember a smell of bleach. I thought Mom had been cleaning and didn't mention it to her." Shudders ran through her. "I was there the next day, Corin. I saw that and shoved it aside as not important."

"At that time, you wouldn't have know that it was important. None of you would have." His heart raised in prayer for his bride, asking for protection for them. "Now that we know this, we can go forward. I won't say anything to your parents, not yet. They don't need to know right at the moment."

"Then, who do we tell? John? He won't believe that his brother did something so awful."

"That's the worry, but we do have to talk to someone." He paused, not quite sure where this would lead, but it would lead somewhere significant he knew.

Darkness finally fell, but they made no move to light any lamps, content just to sit and hold one another and pray. That was the only thing they could do, they decided. It was in God's hands and He would protect them.

# Chapter 17

John stood and watched the young couple as they moved through the church entry the next Sunday morning. He hadn't been back to talk to them, waiting for them to come to him, which they hadn't done. He had been surprised to hear from the Merryville police supervisor, and to hear what had been discovered. It disturbed him greatly, knowing that others had found what he should have. He wasn't happy that his brother had been implicated. He just couldn't see that, but could understand the concerns that were expressed.

Corin knew John was looking for them and he was hoping to avoid the confrontation, and confrontation he knew it would be. Cara hadn't seen John herself but knew he would be around. He always was. She settled down beside Corin, desperately needed a word from God that day.

Cara reached for Corin's hand when the service finished and pulled him away from the crowd and to the front of the church. "Out this way, love. We can avoid most people, I think."

"John being one of them?"

"That's right." She paused. "I know it's not what we should be doing, but right now, after our discussion on Friday, I just can't face him, or Peter. He needs to stay away until he's cleared and I'm not sure who does that or how that happens."

Corin led her to their truck and helped her in, his eyes seeing John walking towards them. He slid behind the wheel and left, leaving John standing dumbfounded behind them. He wasn't sure if Corin had done that on purpose or if he just hadn't seen him.

"John was there?" Cara snuck a look over her shoulder.

"He was, love. I shouldn't have left like that. I'll need to apologize to him." Corin headed for the camp, his eyes watchful, but knowing anywhere along the route, they could be ambushed.

"Now what, Corin? We're not talking to John, we're avoiding Peter, Mom and Dad have to keep their distance, we have a security guard tailing us, and we're homeless."

Corin had begun to grin as she started, finally breaking out in a laugh as she finished. "Hang in there, love. There's a light out there somewhere."

"Yeah, I'm sure there is. I just don't see it. This tunnel is awfully black without it."

Corin shook his head as he parked his vehicle, a frown developing on his face. "I thought we locked the door when we left."

Her eyes shot towards the door. "We did." She sighed. "And our security guard was with us, the other two being off duty. Now what?"

"Stay put." Corin slid from the truck and approached the guard, whose face had darkened as he saw the door. Corin leaned back against the truck, finally moving forward when the guard reappeared, telling Cara to stay put with the doors locked and to hit the horn if anyone approached.

"They've been in here, Corin. They've dismantled the security system, and it's a sophisticated one. I'll need to call Samuel."

Corin followed the guard through the cabin, seeing the tossed appearance of the rooms. "They couldn't have gotten anything. I had it all in my briefcase with me." He spoke in a low voice, low enough the guard bent close as he listened.

Corin was angry. This needed to end and end soon. He followed the guard back out.

"Who do we call then?"

"You'll have to call your local police. I can do that for you seeing as I was the first one in the cabin. But they will want to talk to you." Compassionate eyes followed Corin as he strode towards the truck, anger in his steps.

Cara had the window down. "Corin?"

"They tossed the place, Cara. I have no idea what they were looking for but they tossed it good. We'll have to find somewhere else to stay. John will likely show up. I'll keep you out of it as this will be a report only that the cabin was entered and tossed."

An hour later, John tucked his pen into his pocket and eyed Corin. "What aren't you telling me, Corin?"

Corin shrugged. "Nothing. We came home, found this and are now being moved to a safe house."

"A safe house? By whose authority?"

Corin stood, his eyes stern. "A friend has arranged it for us. We're not telling anyone, not even Cara's family, where we'll be. This has gone on for far too long. It has to end. Cara or I are likely to be the next victim, and we may not survive whatever it is."

John nodded. "I see. Well, then, if that's your decision, we'll have to abide with it. Leave a number you can be reached at."

Corin handed over Blackie's card. "Through him. Cara's family are agreeable to this. I can tell you're not."

"No, I'm not. I'm not sure what to think anymore."

Corin shrugged. "Right now, my only thought is keeping my bride safe and I'll do whatever I need to, within reason, to do just that. Now, if you'll excuse me, I need to get Cara out of here."

He walked away from John, not knowing if he had left a friend or an enemy. Cara moved into his arms, then turned as the guards spoke to them. Corin's briefcase had been searched as had his laptop. Both were clear. They followed the guards to their vehicle and climbed in, Cara's eyes on her parents and brother, not knowing when she would see them again.

Corin turned as Cara touched his back. Samuel had them tucked away in an apartment in town, somewhere safe. He hadn't taken them that far away, leaving the impression that they had gone to Mistletoe. He watched her face, seeing the stress and wanting to relieve it.

"How long do you think, Corin?"

He shrugged. "Blackie was to start his part today, coming looking for us. Samuel hasn't told him exactly where we are, so he'll be working blind. He'll put out that he really needs to talk to you, about the house you're to start." He sighed, not knowing if this was the best route to take. "We'll go from there."

He turned as he heard a tap at the door and then the key turning. A guard walked in, a phone in his hand.

"Samuel asked me to give you this. It's a brand new pay-as-you-go phone. No one but Samuel has the number. His is programmed in, as is our security chief's. Call if you need anything at all." He gave a brief bow of his head and walked back out, locking the door behind him.

"Samuel seems to think of everything, now doesn't he?" Cara moved around the room, knowing she was free to do so with the blackout curtains in place. "This is the building we were thinking of, you know."

"Yes, it is. Let's explore the apartment and see if we could make it work for a while. Now how did he know that?"

Cara shrugged. "I have no idea, Corin. I didn't say anything and I know you didn't."

"He seems to know things. I asked Blackie about that one day, and Blackie said God just tells his father what is needed and where to find it."

"That's an incredible way to live, you know. Could we be like that too?"

Corin dropped an arm around her shoulder. "I suspect that the more we yield to God, the more He speaks to us. But He has special gifts for each one of us, and I would say that is Samuel's gift."

They walked hand in hand through the three-bedroom apartment, seeing the possibilities and downfalls. They finally sat in the kitchen, bare as it was with just the essentials, and talked, agreeing that it would do for now. But when would they be free to live their lives, without hatred and danger dogging their every step? That was the question no one could answer for them.

Corin finally rose, heading for his briefcase and his notes. He wasn't working right now, wouldn't for the next week or so, and that distressed him. He could make plans, diagrams but his clients wouldn't see them, unless he could talk Samuel into having them delivered. And that he was prepared to do. He knew Cara wanted to start work on the house and had been given the information she needed, but they had both been cautioned about using the internet, to keep it to a minimum, to stay away from their email accounts and any other accounts someone could potentially track them through. He didn't like living like this, not one bit.

# Chapter 18

*H*earing a sound at the door, Corin paused, his eyes on the clock. No one should be here. He stepped quietly over to the door and peeked out, seeing John standing there, ready to tap at the door, before he shrugged, then walked away. He frowned. How did John come to be there? He knew Samuel had taken every precaution he could when he set them up here. John shouldn't have known where they were. Samuel had been careful renting the building, having a friend from his home town do just that, leaving no connection between the couple and the apartment.

Cara stood, hands on her chest, her face white as Corin quickly crossed to her.

"It was John. I don't know how he found us. But he left quickly. It's strange. I need to contact Samuel." He kept his voice low before he sent off a quick text, getting a swift reply that Samuel would look into it. They were to stay put. If needed, he would move them again to a new place, but that was risky. "At least, I think it was John. There was something different about him. I can't put my finger on it."

"How did he find us or is he just going from building to building, hoping that he'll come across us?"

"I think that's what he's doing, looking for us. Hopefully, we can flush out Jeremy and Beth's father before they find us. Are you prepared for this?"

She shook her head and turned to pace, her socked feet quiet on the dark hardwood floor. "I fear that, Corin. I really do. I don't want to see either one of us hurt but I know it's a real possibility, isn't it?" She turned, her eyes solemn, as she searched his face.

"It is, love, and I wish it wasn't. All we can do is keep trusting God. He'll get us through it."

"I don't want to lose you, Corin, not when we've just found one another." She almost ran at him, wrapping her arms around him.

"I don't either, but if we do, we'll know God had planned for us to move on and forward, as hard as it will be."

She nodded, her tears soaking his shirt. They stood for the longest time before

Corin's heart opened up and he prayed as he had never prayed before, knowing how close they were to danger and as he prayed, he felt a peace come over them, that God knew what they would face, and no matter how difficult, He would see them through, bringing them out of the fire together.

Corin's phone chimed, bringing them back to the present. He pulled it out and they read it together, Corin's frown deepening.

"This isn't good, Cara. Somehow John has figured out where we are, that we're still in town. He's been calling Samuel repeatedly, saying he wants to talk to us."

"Does he know about Jeremy?"

Corin nodded. "I suspect that he does and that's what this is all about. We can't talk to him." He looked around, knowing they'd be moving. "Samuel's going to get us out of here, to somewhere else he says. That's a danger, love, moving us again."

"At some point, we're going to have to stand and fight, Corin. That we already know."

"I know, but the timing isn't right, not just yet. Gather up what you brought and we'll be ready."

Samuel watched the young couple in his rearview mirror as he drove them away from town that night. He was disturbed. There was no way John should have found them. That he was confident in. He had sent a message to his friend to follow up with the real estate agent, and his friend had done just that, responding that the woman claimed she didn't know she wasn't supposed to tell the police it had been rented by someone from out of town. Samuel would be having a long talk with her about client confidentiality in the near future.

"Where are we heading, Samuel?" Cara's voice reached through to him.

"A little place I know of, between here and Mistletoe. It's isolated, but has good visibility all around. My men are already there. Blackie's been monitoring the traffic around it for us, having called in some friends."

She sighed. "I hate putting people at risk."

Samuel gave her a quick grin, before adding, "It's what we do, Cara. We know the risks and what we're facing."

"I know you do. It doesn't make it easier though."

Corin reached for her hand, finding it cold. "Samuel will do his best, love. That's all we can ask."

They watched with interest as he pulled into a beautiful large home, not what  they had expected.  They waited until he pulled into the garage and then while he checked with his men before he came back and opened the door for them.

"We're here for now.  We may need to move again but if we do, we'll find somewhere to put you two.  Someone is following you too closely for it to be an accident, and that in itself leads me to suspect someone on your town's force.  Who, I have no idea?"

"You suspect John or Peter?"

Samuel nodded, a sad look on his face. "We have to consider that, Cara, no matter how we don't want to.  Now, let's get you inside and settled."

Three days passed, three days that were horribly slow for the couple, the tension in the house rising with each hour.  Cara was growing white and thin, the stress taking her appetite.  Corin kept dreaming up dishes to tempt her to eat. After a few bites, she would just shove them away.

Corin was worried, more worried that he let Cara know. Samuel had been in touch. He had cleared John and Peter, so now the hunt was on for whoever it was that had given away their hiding place. The real estate agent had been horrified to find she had been used like she was. She couldn't even say for sure that it was John who had called her by phone, and that had Samuel questioning everything, including whether Jeremy looked enough like John to pass for him.

Cara knew Corin was worried. She worried about him. This had to end soon, even if she walked away from the security and made herself a target. That, she knew, Corin would never willingly let her do.

Samuel watched the young couple that day, knowing how hard it was for them, and for their families. He knew it had to end soon. He was busy gathering information, as was Simon on his force, and John, who finally conceded that his brother was likely the one after the couple.

He finally approached them, asking them what they had hoped to accomplish with hiding and what they now wanted to do.

Corin stared at him. "I don't know that we wanted to hide. Cara wants to face this monster head on."

Samuel nodded. "I know she does. We're working towards that end. John says he has almost all the reports he needs and his investigation is almost to the point where he can make arrests. He will step back when it's to the crucial point, that he has said. Simon's force has been going over everything John has and will step in at that point."

Cara shook her head. "How did it ever get to here, Samuel? Why has Jeremy never been caught, or Beth's father for that matter?"

"I don't know, Cara. Jeremy has stayed hidden and off the grid for many years. We suspect he's been using a different name. Beth's father? He's been involved in enough legitimate activities that no one would suspect him."

Cara nodded, finally rising from where she had been sitting and pacing away from the men. Corin watched her, knowing her well enough to know she was deep in thought.

"She wants to go home, Samuel. So do I. I know you're doing what is right, keeping us safe, but it's not what we need or want."

Samuel sighed to himself, having already realized this would be their decision. "When did you want to go home?"

"Tomorrow, likely. But not to the cabin. It's too close to family and I don't want them hurt."

Samuel nodded. "I know they're being watched."

Corin gave a quick grin. "The watchers are being watched is what you're saying?" He laughed at Samuel's expression. "Okay, so where can we go? It should be somewhere open. We need to let people know we're back. This can be treated at a honeymoon we never had, but that won't fly."

"No, it won't, not when you two did go away. Let me think on it. I have someone working on a place for you two, knowing this would be your choice." He sighed. "It's coming up to the Christmas season, you know. Let's get you two safe before then."

"That would be my plan, Samuel. Thank you for all you've done."

Samuel shrugged off the thanks and rose, stopping to speak with Cara as he passed her.

Corin watched as Cara continued to pace, waiting for her to come back to him.

She leaned against him as he brought an arm around her, her head down on his. "Samuel says we're going home tomorrow. Is that right?"

"It is, love. It's time, don't you think?"

She nodded. "It is. I don't like it though, not with them still out there."

"I don't either. I want to keep you safe and this isn't how we can do that. But we both know that unless we surface, it will never end."

"And I want you safe. Jeremy will never give up, will he? And Beth's father would always be in the background, watching, haunting us, striking when we least expected it. This way, we'll have control."

"We'll have control over our actions, over who sees us and when, but we can't control them. That's the unknown in all this."

Cara sighed as she slipped down on his knee and he wrapped both arms around her. "That scares me, Corin, more than anything else I have ever expected. I never thought someone would do this to us. I thought being a Christian meant you didn't face difficulties this bad. Guess I was wrong."

"No, not wrong. Some Christians never face what we have or will. God knows how much we can take and will not take us beyond His breaking point for us."

She sighed again, a deep sigh that came from far inside her. "I know that in theory. I just never thought we'd face it in practice."

*Chapter 19*

$\mathcal{T}$he next day, Cara and Corin wandered once more through another home, this one where they planned to stage their fight, to make their last stand against Jeremy. They had openly returned to town, been through the downtown area, gotten the groceries they decided they needed. Cara had spoken with her mother, who in tears had begged her to reconsider their plans. Bruce had said nothing, just that he loved them and to stay safe. Nigel had been vocal, worry for them coming through in his voice and words.

Corin finally stood in the backyard of the house, feeling a sense of having been there, done that, and a sense of foreboding, knowing the end was coming and now that they had set it in process, nothing would stop it.

Cara found him later, drawing him back into the house. She had prepared a meal, that neither felt much like eating. They talked over their plans, including heading into town in the morning. They were on their own, at their request, not willing to put anyone else in danger. Samuel had been against that but had finally agreed to it.

The next morning, Cara and Corin stared at each other as they stood inside the door, getting ready to leave. They had risen early, spent much time in prayer and were now ready to face what they knew was coming. Neither liked the idea but that was life, they decided.

Corin took the keys he was handed for the building they wanted to look at and hand in hand, they walked through the downstairs portion, plans coming together. They had been upstairs already. They finally walked to the local cafe where they were greeted by friends and family, finding it difficult to be among people, knowing they could be hurt because of them.

Corin drove towards their home, knowing he had a tail, but not sure how to shake it. He watched in horror as the car sped up, heading directly for him. He swerved and the car raced by, just missing them. He heard Cara's scream as he slammed on the brakes, then spun the wheel hoping to make it back to town. He watched as the car came back towards him. This time, he had no chance to escape. The resulting crunch of metal and jolt of the impact sent his car flying off the road.   He steered desperately, trying to control their flight, breathing a sigh of relief as the car ground to a halt, just short of a row of trees.   He reached for Cara's hand and pulled her out of the door, having to force his open.

"Come on, love.   We need to hide. They'll be here shortly."

"I know.   That's what they want."   She stared around, even as he pulled her towards the trees.   "This way, Corin.   There's a small path I think we can get to.   It will lead us back to town."   Her breath came in gasps and she hugged her arm to her.   It was only bruised, she thought.

Corin grasped her hand tightly, pulling her along with him, his breathing hard as he tried to listen for pursuers.   "Are you sure about this?"

She nodded.   "There.   It's behind that rock.   No many people know about it."   They slipped behind the rock, their feet slipping slight on the loose stones.   Corin could heard voices shouting from where the car was and prayed that they would make it.

Suddenly, Corin felt himself shoved from behind, flying through the air, his hand letting go of Cara even as she screamed.   He landed heavily, a knee in his back, even as he struggled to rise. His arm was twisted behind him and he was hauled to his feet, shoved forward along the path. He groaned inwardly. They hadn't made it after all, he thought. He had heard Cara scream as he fell and then her voice raised in anger. Then silence fell. Don't let them hurt her, please, dear Lord.

They were shoved through the forest towards a vehicle before blindfolds were slapped roughly across their faces and their hands bound. They felt hands hauling them into a vehicle and throwing them to a floor and then the sound of a door being closed. A van of some kind, Corin thought, but not a passenger van. No, a cargo van of some kind. No one would be looking for a vehicle like that.

Hours later, a patrol officer noticed the skid marks and out of his vehicle, he followed the path of the Corin's car, the broken grass and branches showing in the flickering light from his flashlight. He recognized the vehicle and then started searching, knowing the occupants had escaped but were not to be found. He saw the overlying footprints and grew fearful. He knew Corin and Cara well, having been part of their group at church.

John stood at the roadside, waiting for Peter to return from assessing the area.

"Dad, we'll need to bring in a dog. It looks as if they made it out but were chased. I've kept everyone away from the path they seem to have taken, until we can get Betty and Sherlock in."

John nodded. "I've already made the call. They're about five minutes out. Can you tell if they were hurt?"

Peter shook his head. "I didn't see any blood but that doesn't mean they didn't break something. That's my fear, that they've been hurt enough they can't get away." He looked around. "It looks as if Cara had headed them towards the old Fox trail, hoping to make it to town. I've asked patrol to set up a cruiser there at the other end, but I think we're too late."

John nodded. "I know we are. They left town around three I think someone said. So if that's the case, this happened no later than say a quarter past the hour. That's four hours ago, son." John's emotions go the best of him for a moment. "Where did I go wrong? I never thought Jeremy would do this."

"None of us did, Dad. It's not who we knew him as. But I've been talking to people in town. What he presented to us was not what he showed in town. People were afraid to come forward. Not that they were afraid of you or the force, but they were afraid of Jeremy. I never heard the rumours about that family and his involvement. Did you?”

John shook his head as he watched a truck pull up and the lights turn off, a woman stepping down and then opening the back door of the truck to let out a German shepherd. “Betty’s here. Let’s see what she can find.”

“John? Not how I expected to spend my evening.”

“Me neither, Betty. It’s Corin and Cara that are missing. Their vehicle’s down there but it looks as if they took off from it and were followed.”

“Let me go ahead. How contaminated is the trail?”

“Peter put an officer there as soon as he arrived to keep it clean for you.”

“Thank you, Peter. Now, Sherlock, let’s see what you can find.”

Betty finally stood at the end of the path, Sherlock sitting in his position that indicated the end of a trail. “They were walked to here, from where we saw the scuffle. Loaded into a vehicle, I’d say.”

Peter's light was shining around the tire marks and he frowned. "It's not a light vehicle, Dad. Not a car or a truck. It's more like a van of some kind. Small delivery one, something like that."

"One of those with the roll down doors or two doors on the back, you're thinking?" At Peter's nod, John sighed. "There's been one hanging around town. The driver has been approached and has a reasonable explanation for it. We have the plate number. I'll run it."

"But you don't think it will lead anywhere, do you?"

"No, I don't. The officer who took the number down, did just because he felt uncomfortable with the explanation. He ran them and they came back clean, but we'll need to look at them again." He turned to the canine officer. "Thank you, Betty and Sherlock. We'll be in touch if we need you again."

"Not a problem, John. Sherlock doesn't get the workout he should, so this was good for him."

John paced as he waited for the techs to finish. It was now well past midnight. The couple had been gone for at least ten hours, he thought. Were they even still alive? And who really had them?  He dreaded his visit to Bruce and Emma in the morning and the call he's have to make to Samuel.  This was what they had feared and prayed never happened.

Bruce stood, shock on his face, his hands gripping his hat tightly as he listened to John early the next morning.  He heard sobs from Emma and Nigel's quiet words to his mother.

"This can't be, John.  How?  I thought it was safe for them to come back."

John shook his head, sorrow in his eyes.  "That's what they wanted everyone to think.  They were going on the offensive, hoping to meet them head on out in public.  Whoever has taken them turned the tables on us, and we weren't ready for that."

"Who took them, John?"  Nigel's voice was hard.  "Jeremy?"

John shook his head in sorrow.  "At this point, it's more than likely.  Beth's father as well, we suspect.  It appears now, from what we've learned overnight, that these two have been working together for years, keeping under the radar.  It was only just before I came out here that we received confirmation of that."

"So they could be anywhere? Hopefully still alive?" Emma's voice held hope.

"We pray that, Emma, just that very thing. We'll be leaving officers here with you at all times. If one of you need to leave, call us and we'll have someone escort you. Merryville is sending in officers as well."

Bruce nodded before reaching for his wife and son, bending his head in petition for the safety of his two other children.

John bowed his head as he listened before he silently slipped away. He was angry, more angry than he could ever remember being. He wanted his brother to pay for what he had done. He would hunt him down.

A week had passed since Corin and Cara had disappeared, with no sign of them. There had been no sign of Beth's father either. A cruiser remained parked outside his home around the clock, the officer waiting and watching.

John was fatigued, emotions draining him. Peter was worried about his father who refused to take any time than he absolutely needed from the investigation.

Samuel was in and out of the department, helping where he could, but none of them could track where the couple had disappeared to. That was alarming, given that bodies had been hidden so well for so long in the past.

Bruce finally approached John, a plan in place. John objected but finally agreed. The search teams would start with the property next door to the camp and spread out from there. Prayer groups met daily, petitioning for the young couple's return.

*Chapter 20*

Corin rolled over on the blanket he had been given.  It didn't help much in keeping him warm, didn't help in bringing comfort.  His thoughts went to Cara, as they always did.  He was exhausted, not having had much sleep in the last week.  They had seen to that.  He hadn't seen the head man yet, but he had heard his voice, recognizing how close it sounded to John's.  It had to be his brother.  He had heard his arguments with another man, he assumed likely was Beth's father.

Cara lay asleep on a blanket across the room from him, separated by bars.  They could touch the other's hands but that was it.  He was afraid of how thin she was getting.  He knew she wasn't sleeping, had heard her pacing, her quiet sobs when she thought he was asleep.  It broke his heart to hear and see her like this.  He knew this was being done deliberately, to try and break them.  It just might work, he thought, then prayed for peace and trust and strength, that God would intervene.

He finally heard the words he dreaded, the call for them to be taken out of their cells and brought to the centre room. He stumbled as he was shoved forward, his feet not cooperating with his brain. He heard a whimper from Cara and turned, his hands reaching for her and bringing her to him, seeing the bruises on her arms that he hadn't seen earlier. A dark look crossed his face. Whoever was responsible would pay. He would see to that.

They were stood in the middle of the room, facing away from the entry door. They finally heard the door squeak open and heavy footsteps approached. They refused to turn when instructed to do so, earning Corin a blow to the back that sent him lurching forward, only Cara's hands keeping him on his feet.

They finally heard the voice of the leader, not who they expected at all. Forced to turn and face him, Cara's voice paled with shock.

"You?"

The man nodded. "It is, Cara. Surprised you, didn't I?"

The man was the owner of the land next door, Adam Donaldson by name. He had been a big name in the area for years.

"But why?"

"Why? Because I wanted it all, my dear. Everything I wanted was expensive. Therefore, I turned to crime to finance my lifestyle. Did you really think I made my money the way everyone thought? Of course, I made some, but never enough. Not nearly enough." His coarse laugh shook the heavy weight he carried, cruelty covering his face.

She cringed back from his touch, her face turning away, turning into Corin's shoulder.

"Why did you kill that family?"

"Who? Oh, the bodies you two found. I didn't kill them. Jeremy did. He made a big mistake but covered it up, we thought. Apparently not well enough. He's paid for that mistake. He should have paid years ago."

Cara paled even more, knowing that Jeremy was gone, that John wold never see his brother again, never get to question him. "What did you do to him?"

"Not your affair, young lady." He turned from her before suddenly turning back, a hand smacking across her face, drawing blood from where his heavy ring cut into her lip.

Corin gave a shout of outrage and sprang towards him, his hands on the man's wrist before he could deliver another blow. Cara's screams rang in his ears as blows took him to the floor, where he lay, breathing hard, trying to get his senses back, to stop the spinning in his head. He was hauled to his feet, unsteady, trying desperately to control the heaving of his stomach from the pain and vertigo he now felt. Cara's arms wrapped around him, even as sobs shook her body.

Adam paced in front of them once more, anger driving him. He finally stopped, his eyes on them, trying to come to a decision, but he really didn't know what to do with them. If he killed them, someone would eventually find them. That didn't leave many options. He could sell them into slavery overseas, but that mean an expense of getting them there. He motioned for them to go back to their cells, this time letting them be together. He would taunt them for a while, then make his decision.

He spoke rapidly and in an angry manner to one of the men, who nodded, his eyes on the clock. An hour, he was told, then separate them, bringing Cara to the room across from there, to be kept by herself for a few hours before she was put back into her cell. Adam thought this would break them, make them amenable to whatever he decided to do with them. He little knew the character of the two he had in his control. He would never break them, that he didn't know.

Cara's hands on Corin helped him to lie down, as she ran them over his head and shoulders.

"Corin, are you really okay? You took a beating there."

He nodded, his breath gradually slowing. He reached a hand to touch her face in a gentle manner, to wipe at the tears. "And you?"

"I'm fine, love. This is it, you know. I heard what he said. He's going to put me in another room, one you won't be able to see me in for two hours, then bring me back over there. He thinks it will break us." Her voice was just loud enough for him to hear what she was saying.

"That he will never do, my love. He doesn't know us that well if he thinks that."

"I know. We need to make some plans. How do we escape this, Corin? Will John be able to find us?"

Corin stared at her for a moment, not sure if he should speak. "I don't know that he will. If you get away, run like you've never run before. You need to escape, my love. I'll be behind you, as best I can. It's important that you do that for me. Please?"

She finally nodded, tears tracking down her cheeks. He reached a gentle finger to wipe them away even as he heard the lock opening and felt Cara pulled from him. His hand dropped back to his chest and his eyes closed, a prayer on his heart for his love.

Cara curled up against the wall of the room she was shoved into. Her head rested on her knees, even as she cried out with all her heart for safety, for protection, for escape. It seemed hopeless, Lord, I just can't see how we'll get away. But You are here. You have heard our prayers, have kept us this far. Keep us safe, dear Lord. Bring Corin to safety. Somehow I don't think I'll make it out.

She looked up as the door opened and she was motioned out. She rose, her feet reluctant to move forward even as her body drove her that way. She slumped down on her blanket, her eyes searching for Corin and seeing his form on the blanket on the other side of the bars. He raised his hand slightly, not enough that it would be seen, but enough that she knew he was fine.

Hours later, she had lost track of time. The doors opened again and they were pulled once more from the rooms, but this time shoved through into another room, where Cara was shoved down into a chair in front of a table, Corin made to stand away from her where she couldn't see him.

Adam stood there, leaning meaty hands on the table, a coarse laugh again coming from him.

"You're going to write a suicide note, my dear. A lover's quarrel gone wrong, shall we say?"

She shook her heard. "Never, Adam. Never will I do that. Even if you kill me, I won't do that. People would never believe it."

"Oh, I think they will when I'm done."

She continued to shake her head. "No, they won't. They know me too well. You've lost touch with reality, Adam. You forget what our family is to the community. What you could have been had you chosen differently. May God have mercy on your soul, for you have destroyed so many lives." This earned her another blow across the face, bringing a cry of outrage from Corin, who struggled to get to her, unable to break free of the hands holding him.

Cara turned, her eyes finding his. He saw the calm in her, the peace, and knew she had made her decision. She would not give in. He knew what that meant and despaired, but then steeled his heart. He needed to find that peace and confidence as well. Lord, this is where I really need You to step in. This is it for us. I can't see us going on from here, from getting away.

Little did he know that even as Adam continued his demands, with Cara refusing each one, even as he struggled against the hands holding him to find release and get to her, that the authorities had found them and were putting their plan into place, moving in to surround the building, to take out the men stationed outside, to quietly slip inside the old mill and search, taking down any man they found.

Cara finally shoved back from the table and stood, her stance straight and confident. "It won't work, Adam. You can't intimidate me. You tried to kill me by electrocution but God stepped in. He sent His angel to bring healing, to bring help, to bring comfort. I saw Saul, as did others. He won't let you destroy us, not unless He wills it is time for us to come home. And somehow I don't have that answer, that our time on earth is not done. Do what you will. I will not sign any suicide note."

Adam's anger was to the point that foam speckled his lips as he raged, finally turning his weapon towards Corin. Cara shook her head, her eyes on Corin, knowing that he shared her belief. She screamed as a shot ran out and Corin flew backwards, to lie still, blood covering his chest. She tried to get to him, but arms surrounded her from behind, locking hers to her body, and lifting her, fighting and screaming, her hands clawing at the arms holding her, her feet kicking at whatever they could reach. Adam pointed towards the door, motioning for the man to carry her out of the room and down to the vehicle. He had a plan for her now, a plan that would destroy her family as well.

The man stumbled as he walked down the steps, Cara fighting him every step of the way. He froze as he felt a weapon against his neck, stopping where he was, his arms still locked around a fighting Cara. His arms were pried from her and she was picked up and carried from the room, fighting at first until she recognized Peter's voice. She turned her face into his shoulder and sobbed, crying out that they had killed Corin.

Peter sat her down finally in an ambulance, his arms still around her, trying to comfort her, to get her to let the paramedics examine her.  She stopped fighting, her body going stiff at first, then lax, as she went into shock.  The paramedic spoke quietly to Peter and he helped her lie back on the stretcher, seeing the paramedics begin their assessment of her, his eyes tracing back to the mill, hearing the sound of gunfire and shouts, finally silence ringing through the air.  He moved out of the vehicle, his eyes on the building, waiting.

Cries came for paramedics and the second team that was on standby grabbed their kits and ran forward, not sure what they would find, but knowing there would be injured to attend to.

John pointed to them.  "In there.  There are some with wounds that can wait.  Corin can't.  He's been shot in the chest.  He needs help now."  He turned as an officer approached, asking how Cara was.

"Peter's with her.  She's gone into shock.  He says she thinks Corin's dead."

John nodded in a grim manner.  "He may yet be.  They're working on him."  He returned to stand over the paramedics as they scrambled to stop the blood, to assess Corin's vitals, to get lifesaving fluid running into his body from an IV.  A shout from them sent men scrambling for a stretcher. Finally, they lifted him and carried him out. John frowned, counting heads. There was an extra man there, one he didn't know. The man turned, the dying sun reflecting off his white hair and beard as he nodded to John, his hand raised to him.

John paused, not quite sure what he had seen. He had heard Cara and her family speak of the man who had appeared all those months ago, who was there and then not there. He ran after the men, not surprised to see that the man was gone. He stopped his forward race, his eyes raising to the heavens. Lord, I do believe I just saw your angel, here once more for my friends. Thank you.

Corin's stretcher was shoved into the rig and then the rig raced away, taking him to lifesaving aid and surgery. Peter climbed back in the rig beside Cara, knowing that was where he needed to be.

He met Bruce, Emma and Nigel as they ran towards him, tears on their faces, as he stood inside the doors of the Emergency Department.

"Peter?" Bruce's cry broke his heart.

"We have them, Bruce. They're alive. Corin's in surgery. He was shot in the chest but I'm told it missed anything vital. Lot of bleeding. Cara's fine. She's in shock, of course, beaten, thin, tired, worn out. She said she saw Corin shot and thought she had lost him. I was with her when she said that. I had managed to get her away. Come on. They want you with her."

Peter led the way, then stood back, his heart breaking for his father. It had been confirmed that the body they had found earlier that day was his uncle. He didn't know how his father would cope now.

# Chapter 21

Cara sat beside Corin three weeks later, their hands joined, not wanting to let one another go or let the other out of their sight. She could hear her mother moving around in the kitchen, preparing a meal to thank those who had helped them. It was a happy day but a sad one. John had been by earlier.

He had brought news that Jeremy had in fact been driving the car when it had gone off the road, killing the family. That had not been the intent. In a panic, he had helped to bury the family and then unable to handle being around the camp, had left town. The young man with him, they had never learned his name, had left as well. That was an investigation that was over as far as it could be.

John couldn't apologize enough for what Jeremy had put the family through. He felt responsible even though he had been told he could not have helped what had happened, that Jeremy had made his decision and lived to die for it.

Beth's father had been arrested as well, his carefully built empire tumbling down around him as his activities of money laundering, extortion, blackmail, and drugs came to light. Her mother had quietly packed up and left, not wanted in the town any more. Tam and Beth had been found, having been kept captive by Adam and used as a weapon against Beth's father, to keep him in line. They were finally able to make peace with Cara and move on. Tam returned to his life overseas while Beth had disappeared, not saying where she was headed. Cara really didn't want to know. Everything they had gone through had been orchestrated by Adam. He had watched Cara that day so long ago as she had washed the blood from the steps, thinking she had found them out and had made plans to remove her, plans that had waited until now.

Corin and Cara had shared a look when John told them about the man he saw, a smile covering their faces.

"It was Saul, John." Corin had finally spoken. "I do believe he was an angel, sent just for us. He may well have been one of our guardian angels. If that's the case, he had his hands full, didn't he?"

Nigel had hugged his sister when she finally walked into the house that day, not wanting to let her go, but knowing that she was with the one God had meant for her, had planned for her all those years ago. He had found his own love over the summer, a lady he had known for years, who finally agreed to date him and then to marry him. Their wedding was planned for the new year, after the Christmas rush was over. And what a Christmas it would be this year, so full of thanksgiving.

Bruce had nodded when Corin tried to apologize for not keeping Cara safe, merely stating that he knew Corin's heart and that what had happened could not have been avoided, that God had been with them each step of the way.

Cara lifted her head from where she had rested it on Corin's shoulder, seeing the fatigue still in his face, but the bright light of joy and strength. She reached to kiss his cheek, bringing his face around.

"Cara, I love you, more than I ever thought I could. God has been good to us. This is one Christmas I intend to enjoy. Mom and Dad are on their way, should be here within a couple of hours. Our friends and family are here, and I have the love of my life in my arms."

She snuggled closer, sharing his sentiments and knowing that no matter what they faced in the future, God was there in the centre of it all. He had brought them to the precipice of their trust in Him and kept them from falling over, bringing them back from the edge to serve Him.

# *Epilogue*

*C*hristmas Day dawned bright and clear, the sun sparkling off the light snow that had fallen over night. Corin stamped his feet as he entered the house they had bought just a week or so ago, deciding that apartment living was not for them after all. He was on a hunt for his bride, not finding her.

He finally tracked her down in the room they had designated as their office, her hands running across the beautiful oak desk John had given them, saying it was little enough that he could do for them. He watched as a smile crossed her face before he walked towards her, encircling her with his arms, turning her to face him and claiming his Christmas kiss.

She leaned back. "I think I like Christmas more now than I did even as a kid."

He laughed, the glad sound ringing through the room. "I'm glad of that. Christmas certainly has a new meaning for us, now doesn't it?"

She nodded, her hand finding his and leading him back to their living room, to the tree she had put up a few days ago. She reached for the ornament he had given her, to celebrate their first Christmas together.

"I like this, love. It's so you."

He nodded, his arms surrounding her, his chin resting on her shoulder. "It's so true, what it says."

She smiled. "That it is. Where do we go from here, Corin? We can't just live our lives to ourselves any more, not with what God has brought us through."

"No, we can't. We need to pray about that and see where He leads us. It will be a mission field, not matter where we are or what we do. And I get to spend that with the love of my life and my best friend."

Dear Readers:

Thank you for choosing to pick up the story of Cara and Corin. This was another in a challenge to write a 50,000 word novel during National Novel Writer's Month, the month of November.

It was also a challenge to write as the characters couldn't quite decide what they wanted but one thing I knew. It had to show how God keeps us safe, even when we're walking through darkness or along a cliff where danger and death waits before.

Tornadoes are something that really scare me and few weather events do. They are destructive, taking lives and property and forever changing those who go through them. In May 1985 I lived in Barrie, Ontario, Canada. On that day an EF4 tornado swept through my town, part of a series of tornadoes that day. Eight people lost their lives that day, six with a block of where I lived. We were just on the edge of the path, a hundred feet closer and we may not have survived. God brought us through that day, just as He does with whatever we face. That is a promise I cling to.

Courage comes in many forms. But God has promised that He is with us every step of our lives. Sometimes courage is just stepping through a door. Sometimes it's facing life-threatening illness or events. Never doubt that for a moment.

As I close, may you know that God loves you so much, that He has promised never to leave you on your own, that His promises never fail.

God bless each one of you. No one knows the journey that each one of us faces. That journey can take twists and turns no one ever counted on. It has for me.

Oh, Saul - how can I forget him? Was he an angel or not? Do you believe that people can come and go that quickly? I have seen a flash of light around my car, protecting me. I have had unknown dogs walk me home and then disappear. Who's to say if that was an angel sent from God for just the purpose of protection? We do not know the ways of God, can't know them. I firmly believe that He protects us in every way and that He will send us protection in the manner that we need at the time we need it.

Ronna